Blueburrie

Ray Ferch

R1

Ray Ferch Press

Dedicated to my wife and son
who make me laugh every single day.

Special thanks to my 12th grade English teacher
(who's name I can't remember at the moment)
for telling me my short story was really good.

Chapter One

A Perfect Day

In a small town, in a small area of the world, lied a town that was nearly perfect by any sense of the word. Despite the year being 528 AD, deep in the dark ages, the small town of Blueburrie, was the happiest place on earth. Everyone was happy. Everything was perfect, and most importantly, all things were safe.

In the middle of the town was a perfect castle, painted blue. Blueberry trees, bushes, and scrubs surrounded not only the Castle, but were also seen throughout the city. The streets were stained of the fallen blue berries. Blue birds, blue jays and peacocks flew while blue crawfish, and blue gills swam in ponds. All houses located within the city limits were painted blue. All shops and entertainment venues, blue. And finally, the most important part of the city, the city wall, quarried from lapis, a majestic blue stone.

The city wall is what made Blueburrie so special. Nearly twenty-eight feet tall, the wall provided numerous features that kept everyone safe and sound. The first five feet was sanitized and washed hourly. The middle of the wall was the thickest to protect from any outside enemies. The top of the wall was covered in razor sharp timber weeds. Yet, what made that wall so special, was the fact that it was built around every home, farm, and shop in the city. Normally in medieval times, the city walls only protected the royalty. Blueburrie was different, every single resident was guaranteed the protection of that wall. No one was allowed in, and no one was allowed out without the Queen's permission.

Ruled by The Queen Mary, who insisted happiness, perfection, and safety would be assured for all who live in her city. She prided herself on befriending everyone. So much so that right in the middle of the town square was a large wooden sign that said, "The Queen Mary's Friends: Two hundred and twenty-six," As people had children the number would raise, and unfortunately declined when people passed.

It was the first Saturday in October, the year 528 A.D.. A fine autumn day, the day promised a slew of activities within the walls of Blueburrie. Near the butcher shop, a peacock was being roasted for The Queen Mary's ball. "I think peacock tastes like chicken," said Blur.

"What's chicken?" asked Hu.

"It's like a small Peacock but not as beautiful," said Blur. Located outside the butcher shop hung a sign, "Blur's Butcher Shoppe," Blur had been a butcher his whole life. His nephew Hu was twenty-three years old and was promising to take over the family business someday.

"I know most people don't like the claws, but I think they're the tastiest part of the peacock," said Hu.

"I agree," said Blur.

As the sun started to peek over the city wall the sudden cackle of one of the local peacocks could be heard. Far down third street was the small cobble home of Ray McJohnson. One of The Queen Mary's friends and resident of Blueburrie. Ray was a tapper in The Queen Mary's entertainment division. His primary job was to do his very best to provide the very best tap-dancing entertainment that The Queen Mary requested. "Today is going to be a perfect day," Smiled Ray while wiping the sleep from his eyes. Hopping out of his bed, he slid right into his tap shoes, perfectly shined. "Damn. If these aren't the best tap shoes I've ever owned," Ray grinned. "Wait until the royal court hears my tappers. The Queen Mary is going to love all my new steps." Just as Ray finished brushing his hair, a knock at the door.

"Good morning Ray, I made you breakfast. Blueberry waffles with peacock link sausage right from Blur's Butcher Shoppe," said Flounder.

"That sounds delicious. I always look forward to your breakfasts in the morning," said Ray. Flounder and Ray had been acquaintances since birth. Born on the same day from different mothers, Ray and Flounder were practically brothers. They lived next door to each other. They went to school together, sat next to each other, and even had their first job together as blueberry bush trimmers. Their lives started to drift apart in their early twenties when Ray realized he wanted to tap dance professionally. Flounder didn't have the skills Ray was blessed with, but it didn't matter to him. He was just happy to associate with Ray and was always happy for him. Flounder, on the other hand, thought of himself as having very few skills. His father had always wished he would take over the family locksmith business, but Flounder just couldn't grasp the concept of picking locks, locking mechanisms, or keys. He struggled with why locks were needed in the first place. The city of Blueburrie was so safe and protected by their great city wall, why did people need locks on their doors? Thought Flounder.

"We should probably leave soon. I need to get to tap dance practice," said Ray.

"Can I come too and watch?" asked Flounder.

"Of course. I love when you cheer me on," said Ray. The two left and headed towards the town square.

High in the castle, The Queen Mary awoke staring at a beautiful mural that she had painted earlier that week of a peacock spreading its feathers. Near her nightstand lay a pile of recently painted cards of portraits of her friends. "Oh, this is a lovely portrait of Flounder," she muttered. Flipping to the next portrait in her pile was a portrait of Gimlett and Morehouse, twins born a few weeks earlier. "My new friends. They have hair like their mother, semi-supple," The Queen Mary said under her breath. She flipped through the remaining cards to find a portrait of a blueberry, a portrait of a blueberry bush, a portrait of another blueberry. "Lots of blueberries this morning," The Queen Mary said. Finally, one card left. There stood Ray in his shiny tappers. "Ah, Ray. I can't wait to hear that beautiful tapping. Oh, how it brings me such joy. That tapping sound."

"Margarine," The Queen Mary bellowed. "I'm awake. Bring me my blueberry donut, and coffee. Oh, and throw some blueberry juice in my coffee to sweeten it," Margarine now running from the castle kitchen below.

"Were there any good portrait cards this morning?" asked Margarine.

"There was a beautiful portrait of a blueberry. There was also a portrait of Ray. My how he looks debonair in his tappers," said The Queen Mary.

"What color was the blueberry?" asked Margarine.

"Blue," responded The Queen Mary.

"I meant what shade," said Margarine.

"Light," said The Queen Mary.

****

"I think we're really in a good position to get the best flowers possible. If we harvest them early enough, we should be able to have them ready for the ball at peak blooming," said Pom. "We can cut the flowers, collect them, and bundle them," explained Pom.

"It honestly sounds like a good plan, but I don't think that's going to work," said Gil.

"You're probably right," said Pom. The local flower shop was handed down through the generations to a small statured man, named Gil. Once his great grandfather's flower shop, Gil was given the shop after his father and grandfather died in the terrible battle of five hundred and two. In the fog of war, Gil's grandfather and father were riding bare back on the same horse. An arrow from a crossbow pierced the skin of a nearby drummer boy, his screech startling the horse. It ran in to a nearby swamp and bucked Gil's father and grandfather. They fell directly into a small pond full of black mold. Little did they know they had an allergy to black mold. After three days of sitting in the swamp, Gil's father and grandfather passed away. "The black mold was probably the cause of death," Dr Dunston said, Blueburrie's chief doctor.

****

"Damn it. I just stepped in more peacock shit. My tappers," yelled Ray. "Suzin is supposed to be the town street cleaner. Why doesn't he keep his promises? Now I have peacock shit stuck in the middle of my tappers and they don't have that crisp sound," Ray mumbled.

"Sometimes it's hard to tell the blueberries from the peacock dung," said Flounder. "I think it's going to be a huge ball tonight," said Flounder. "I walked past Blur's Butcher shop this morning and they were roasting that big pig of a peacock we saw walking around the other day."

"They caught him?" Ray said.

"You bet they did. I love the way roasting peacock smells in the morning. My favorite part is the ankles," said Flounder.

"Me too," said Ray.

Chapter Two

PREPARATIONS

∾o∾

The town square started to become busy with excitement preparing for the big party that night. The Queen Mary wanted to welcome her two new friends, Gimlett and Morehouse, to her ever-growing list of friends. Blue flags were being raised around the community dance floor. The stage was being decorated with blueberry paint, and cloth lanyards. Beautiful peacocks walked around the grounds spreading their wings and strutting majestically. Despite their beauty, they did leave a mess of scat littered around the outdoor dance floor. Suzin was rest assured it would all be cleaned up before the night of the big event. When asked if he would clean it up he simply said, "I will."

"Does anyone know if Gil is bringing the flowers?" Mosh inquired. "I swear that guy is an idiot. He does everything wrong. If I was in charge of fresh flowers, I would have had them picked and ready to go by now. Where is this guy? Did anyone talk to Pom? What is the point of even decorating if both of these guys are going to be moronic about how they handle decorating this venue? I swear, every ball we go through this with these guys." Mosh persisted to get angrier and angrier. "I care too much. I care TOO much. I simply cannot deal with this level of incompetence," said Mosh while he stormed towards Gil's Flower Shop.

"I decided to wash the wheelbarrow," Pom said. "I was looking over the undercarriage and it looked like the sand we used on the last job really caused some havoc on that wheelbarrow. I also was inspecting our sun-dried blueberries. They don't look as sun dried as I think I'd like them. This is going to be a problem in the future, because I know the sun-dried blueberries are The Queen Mary's favorite," said Pom.

"All great information," said Gil. "Did you manage to cut any flowers for The Queen Mary's ball?"

"No," replied Pom. "I was too busy with the wheelbarrow and the sun-dried blueberries. Did I mention that they aren't as sun dried as I'd like them to be?" Just as Gil was going to respond, Mosh stormed into the store.

"Where's the fucking flowers?" Mosh screamed.

"I haven't had a chance to cut them yet," Pom explained. "I was looking over our wheelbarrow and realized it was incredibly dirty."

"So what?" Mosh said. "Did you need the fucking wheelbarrow to cut flowers? Do you understand that The Queen Mary loves flowers at her balls and now we have none. Why in the name of the Almighty would you be cleaning your wheelbarrow and staring at sun dried blueberries when you KNEW you had to cut the flowers?" Pom blankly stared at Mosh. He had every intention of picking the flowers, but just got distracted with other tasks.

"You guys are morons. I need those flowers. I'll find another solution. You know this isn't my first ball. I've been organizing balls for over five years. The Queen Mary wouldn't have named me Chief Ball Manager for nothing" said Mosh, slamming the door and nearly slipping on the peacock scat-soaked sidewalk.

****

"You know what Ray? I think I got the last piece of Peacock scat out of your tapper. I don't even smell anything anymore on the bottom of your shoes," Flounder said as Ray lie on his back with his legs spread eagle in the air.

"Flounder, I'm glad I can always count on you to help. Now that my tappers are back on track, let's head to the square. I simply must practice."

Flounder and Ray took off running down the street, clacking and smacking as Ray's newly cleaned tap shoes made that sweet sound The Queen Mary craved. As they ran past the stables, they saw Suzin resting against a chair. "Hi Suzin. By the way, I stepped in some Peacock shit this morning. Any chance you'll clean that up before the ball?"

"I will," replied Suzin.

Back in the castle, Margarine laid out The Queen Mary's schmock, hose, kirtle, dress, belt, surcoat, girdle, cape, and hood. Each piece pressed early in the morning and sprayed with fresh blueberry scent. "I just love balls," Margarine said as she rubbed her hands over the freshly pressed girdle. "It's going to be huge. It's not every day that I'm able to make two friends in a single day. This calls for a ball of enormous size. I'm so excited to meet my new friends Gimlett and Morehouse," The Queen Mary smiled as she thumbed through some new portrait cards that were painted several minutes earlier. "Blueberry, Blueberry, Blueberry on Toast, oh here's a cute portrait of Suzin eating a blueberry," she said.

"Anything else interesting?" asked Margarine, unlacing the girdle.

"No, just a portrait of Pom washing the underside of his wheelbarrow. That thing art nasty," The Queen Mary joked.

"Ha," said Margarine. "You are so funny."

"I know I am," The Queen Mary said while gazing out the Castle window at the town square below. She noticed the friend sign. "Two hundred and twenty-eight friends. Pretty impressive. Everyone in this town is my friend. Good friend. Best friend even. I sometimes lie awake at night thinking about all my friends. What are they doing? I wonder what they're saying about me. I wonder if they want to dress like me. Be like me. It sometimes really stresses me out. Being so popular. How many friends do you have Margarine?"

"None," she said.

"Margarine. That's not true. You have me, I'm your one and only friend. I'll always be your friend. You don't need other friends," The Queen Mary stated.

"I suppose you're right," sighed Margarine.

"Of course, I'm right. I'm The Queen Mary. And you're just Margarine."

****

"I just can't believe that my flowers aren't going to be ready. How many times have I asked those morons to cut flowers early so we have them ready in time?" Mosh grumbled to himself as he walked down 5th street towards the city center. Clack Clack Smack Smack, he began to hear clacking sounds getting closer and closer to him.

"Mosh. Mosh. How are you?" screamed Flounder.

Oh God, not these assholes, I swear I could entertain The Queen Mary better than them, thought Mosh. "How are you Flounder? Ray? Doing well I assume."

"Doing great," said Flounder. "We were just on our way to the square to practice Ray's routine. You know the ball is tonight?" asked Flounder.

"Of course, I know it's tonight, you moron. I'm in charge of everything. The Queen Mary promoted me several months ago to Chief Ball Manager. I pretty much have to do everything around here. Did you talk to Purk and his band? I wonder if his tuba is clean," said Mosh.

"His what?" asked Flounder.

"His Tuba. His Tuba. His instrument. The thing he blows in," Mosh said as he waves his arms and hands around.

"Oh you mean his Bladder Pipes," said Flounder.

"Tuba, Bladder Pipes, whatever. Did he get them fixed? If we don't have any music tonight, I doubt you'll have any clacking or smacking to do with those fancy tap shoes of yours," said Mosh.

"I think Purk said he needed to exercise the bladder on his bladder pipes," said Ray.

"Exercise. That's the last thing I need right now," said Mosh. "So now I need to cut flowers, decorate, and exercise Purk's bladder pipes for this thing tonight. Unreal. Don't step in any Peacock shit, it seems to be all over the place. Where's Suzin?" yelled Mosh as he stormed off towards the Stable.

"That guy really needs to settle down," Ray said. "I get it. Balls can generate a lot of pressure, but he doesn't have to yell at people all the time. Things in life tend to happen for a reason. Remember how my cousin Toss always liked telling us what to do as kids?" asked Ray.

"Yeah," Flounder said. "Well, he never stopped telling everyone what to do. He loved being a great leader. Always forcing us to play a certain way. He would tell us when to go to bed, when to eat our blueberries, when and where to sit. The guy had that great knack for demanding things." said Ray.

"Yeah," said Flounder.

"And looked at what happened? Like perfect timing in life, the Dominades called upon Toss and he KNEW being a Dominator was going to be perfect for him. Finally, he could tell even more people in life what to do and what to believe in," said Ray.

"Yeah. How is your cousin Toss doing? I heard he might be coming home for fall break soon," said Flounder.

"Depends on the conversions. If he gets his numbers in before the end of October, he'll be able to come home. I would love to see him," said Ray.

"Here's hoping," said Flounder.

Meanwhile, the town really began to come alive. All of The Queen Mary's friends were busy getting ready for the big ball. As the peacock roasted in Blur's Butcher Shop, a team of Blueberry pickers gathered their buckets for the mid-morning pick. Several teams of Blueberry Bush Trimmers, otherwise known throughout the city as BBT's were hard at work, snipping and trimming bushes for the big ball. Exterminators perched high in tree tops and lookout towers, keeping a sharp eye out for any birds that weren't blue colored in nature. Near the stables all horses were having their coats and manes stained with fresh blueberry juice.

Mosh was pleased to see no sign of Suzin when he first approached the stables. Maybe he was finally out cleaning peacock dung like he promised, thought Mosh. He saw one of The Queen Mary's friends brushing a small blue pony. "Have you seen Suzin?" inquired Mosh.

"I think he's working from home."

"Working from home? How the hell can he clean up peacock shit, if he's working from home? You've got to be kidding me," Mosh screamed. "When I saw Suzin earlier, he said he was going to clean up Peacock shit before the ball," The Queen Mary's friend simply shrugged and went about brushing his pony. "I swear. First, I have to pick flowers, then decorate, then I'll have to fix Purk's bladder pipes and now I have to clean up peacock shit? How the fuck am I supposed to do all of this?" yelled Mosh, marching out of the stables. "This day will never end. What's next?"

"I don't think that'll work," Gil said. He was watching Pom try and use a small brush to clean the under carriage of the wheelbarrow. "I mean, don't get me wrong. I think it's a good idea, I just don't think it's going to work in this situation," Gil walked over to his desk and started to look through some wheelbarrow portraits. "You see these are what new wheelbarrows look like," Gil said, showing Pom a portrait of a brand-new wheelbarrow.

"Can we get a new wheelbarrow?" asked Pom.

"No, we simply can't afford one right now. I just wish our old wheelbarrow looked new like these," said Gil. Pom continued to try and scrub some of the sand from beneath the wheelbarrow. He scrubbed in a circular motion until beads of sweat started appearing on his skin and his arm cramping.

"I told you that you were doing it wrong," said Gil.

"Well, if I don't get the sand off of here, I'll never get around to cutting those flowers for the ball," Pom said. Both Gil and Pom sighed as they stare at the wheelbarrow that had nothing to do with the task of cutting flowers.

"This is a problem," said Gil.

"You aren't kidding," said Pom.

Mosh opened the door to Blur's Butcher Shoppe to find Hu standing behind the counter. "Hu. Just the man I wanted to see," said Mosh.

"I can help you in just a second. Please take a numeral," scolded Hu. Grumbling under his breath, Mosh grabs the next numeral.

"DXXVIII," shouted Hu.

"That's me," said Mrs. Warwick. "Do you have any Bluegills?"

"Sure do," said Hu.

"Are they fresh?"

"Sure are," Hu claims.

"I'll take three. I mean, four. Do you have any Blue Fin Tuna?" asks Mrs. Warwick.

"We sure do."

"Are they fresh?" inquired Mrs. Warwick.

"Fresh as of this morning. Big ones too. Extra Blue," said Hu.

"Are they fresh?" said Mrs. Warwick not hearing Hu the first time.

"Yes. Yes they are."

"I think I'll pass. I like my blue fin tuna slightly blue, not extra. Anyway. I'll take four pounds of ground peacock and four bluegills. Is that peacock rump roast I smell?" asked Mrs. Warwick.

"No, that's a whole bird we have roasting for the big ball tonight. Are you going?"

"Going where?" asked Mrs. Warwick.

"To the ball? Are you going to the ball tonight?"

"Oh. I don't like balls as much as I used to. What with all the kids dancing and prancing and singing. Not to mention Ray and his tapping. His tap dancing gives me fever rashes," claimed Mrs. Warwick.

"Oh that's terrible. Well. That'll be four Piloncitos," said Hu.

"Four? The price of everything is so expensive these days. Ever since we started sending more of our boys to the Dominades, I swear everything costs more. I just wish those non-believers would convert and we'd be done with this. Four Piloncitos. I swear," Mrs. Warwick grabbed her meat and scurried past Mosh out of the store.

Mosh, now pacing back and forth. His face red with anger. "How much fucking longer do I have to wait?"

"DXXIX," said Hu.

"Me," yelled Mosh. "Listen. I overheard you talking about that peacock you've got roasting. How's it going? Are you ready for tonight? You know, I have a lot of people counting on this food. They've been smelling that pig of a peacock roast all morning long," said Mosh.

"Yeah . . . here's the thing," Hu said. "It's such a large peacock, we have to keep juicing it. And the store has been so busy this morning I haven't been able to juice it as much as I'd like. I'm afraid it's going to be dry."

"What do you mean 'dry'? Where's Blur? Why can't he help?" Mosh said, his face turned a different shade of red.

"Blur's slurring."

"Slurring? What do you mean 'slurring'?" said Mosh.

"He's drunk. He started drinking ale this morning and he's drunk. He's pre-ballin' it," said Hu.

"So, he can't juice the peacock because he's too drunk?" yelled Mosh.

"He'll over juice," said Hu.

"Damn it. So, I have to cut the flowers, decorate the square, fix the pipes, pick up peacock shit, and NOW I have to make sure someone juices the peacock so it doesn't get dry. How the hell am I supposed to do all of this? It's too much," yelled Mosh before he stormed out of the butcher shop.

****

"Your hair is so soft and shiny," said Margarine. She was brushing The Queen Mary's hair.

"I know. It's my royal heritage. My mother's, mother's daughter had such soft hair that people would talk about it constantly. She used to sell it and people would make shirts and slacks from her soft supple hair. Do you think my hair is soft and supple enough to make slacks?" asked The Queen Mary.

"Of course. You could even make schmocks and socks with your hair," said Margarine.

"I know. My hair is gorgeous," The Queen Mary grabbed a fresh stack of portraits next to her lounge chair. "Peacock, Peacock feathers, Blueberry, Bluegill, Peacock Roasting, Oh here's a good portrait of Blur with a pint of ale from this morning. He looks so happy. He must be getting excited for the ball. I simply can't wait for the peacock he's roasting. I just love the cheeks. Don't you?" asked The Queen Mary.

"Me too," said Margarine.

****

"My Almighty. We need to cross the street and there's just so much . . ."Ray began to exclaim.

"Dung," finished Flounder. Ray looked on to the street with despair.

"I can't be late. I just can't be late. If I'm late for tap practice, I'll never be ready for the big ball tonight," Ray started to tear up. "My paradiddle. I need to practice my paradiddle. I just don't have the steps down. If I get any more peacock shit on my shoes, I'll never get to practice. Oh. What's the point?" Ray said with tears fully flowing now.

"Ray, do a handstand," yelled Flounder.

"What?"

15

"Just do a handstand. Do it now. I will carry you across the street. We'll get those tappers as high as we can, so you won't get an ounce of dung on your beautiful shoes," Flounder said.

"Flounder, you're a genius," Ray said. He jumped on his hands and did a perfect handstand. Flounder approached him from behind and grabbed his waist. "You're going to have to direct me, Ray. I can't see with your butt in my face."

"Forward," screamed Ray.

The sound of blueberry juice combined with peacock dung squished through Flounders toes as he took that first step into the street. Having never learned how to wear shoes, Flounder was accustomed to the sound. "Forward. Keep moving forward," commanded Ray. "You're doing great. Keep moving. We're so close to the other side." Flounder's feet now covered in a sludge of peacock dung and blueberry juice. His legs shook and he tried to keep Ray from falling into the street.

"Toss me, Flounder. Toss me." Flounder reached down to grab a hold of Ray's shoulders, And with all his might sent him straight up into the air. With a flip, Ray landed perfectly on the other side of the street.

"Did someone say 'toss'?" the voice of a mysterious man came out of the shadows. Ray turned and caught site of his long loss cousin, Toss, back from the Dominades.

"Toss.. You son of a peahen. How the hell are you? Back from the Dominades? How was it? Did you kill any non-believers? How many people did you convert?"

"All in good time, my simpleton cousin. All in good time," said Toss as he gazed over and looked at Flounder still standing in the middle of the street. "Hi Flounder. Nice to see you. Well. Just don't stand there in the middle of the street with peacock shit on your feet. Come with me, I've got a tale to tell."

Chapter Three

Toss' Tale

L eading Ray and Flounder to a nearby pavilion, Toss was a man of significant size. Standing at nearly five foot one, he was nearly a foot taller than most of The Queen Mary's friends. Toss' forearms were larger than his calves and his eyes were yellow like the sun. His head was large, which indicated to all he had an enormous brain. His beard was long and braided in to two separate pig tails. He wore panda-skin slacks, alligator boots, snakeskin gloves, and a shirt made from llama hair. His helmet was made of elephant bone and his belt was camel hair.

"Come on boys. Flounder, you sit over there. Your feet smell like shit," said Toss.

"No problem, I'm just excited to see you," Flounder said.

"I guess my tap practice can wait," said Ray.

"Of course, it can. Well, sit back and let me tell you about my tale," Toss boasted as he kicked off his alligator boots.

"You have a tail?" Flounder said with look of shock on his face.

"Not a tail. You simpleton. A Tale. Tale. As in T-A-L-E."

"Oh. Tale," said Flounder, still unsure of whether Toss had a tail.

"As you guys know, I'm a Dominator with The Queen Mary's elite section of the Dominator Conversion Program or the DCP. You haven't seen me for several years, simply because I've been so busy converting and/or killing anyone that doesn't believe. It hasn't been easy, let me tell you. But I've really excelled at this and I'm really proud of what I do. Every day I make the world a safer place by forcing my beliefs. Sure, people can have their own opinions. But I know my opinions are right, and really are the only option. Any questions?"

Flounder and Ray looked at each confused, but also amazed at the tale Toss was telling. "Where did you get those boots?" ask Flounder.

"Oh, these old things? Well, they're alligator for one. A very rare and dangerous beast that lives outside the city walls. I didn't ACTUALLY kill an alligator to get them, but I did take them off a dead non-believer's body."

"What's it like outside the city walls? The Queen Mary never lets us out," said Ray.

"Dangerous. Very dangerous. When the wild beasts aren't chasing you, the non-believers are trying to force their beliefs upon you. There are snakes, and bees, and wild chickens, and a moose and mid-sized cats. Beasts of all types. There are berries that will make you sick, and large areas of sand known as deserts. There's large bodies of water, with crashing waves, and when you take a drink, it tastes so salty you can't even quench your thirst no matter how much you drink."

"Sounds horrific," said Ray

"It is and it isn't. That's the thing. I never feel so alive when I'm outside the city walls of Blueburrie. Yeah, there's so many dangerous things, but there's so many amazing things too. One time I heard a bear fart in the woods. I suspect he was going to take a shit, but he got too embarrassed and ran off. This other time I fell down something called a sink hole. I was stuck there for days, until I figured out a way to climb out. I have even eaten a cranberry," bragged Toss.

"You mean a blueberry," said Flounder.

"No. A CRAN-berry," Toss said as he started to reach into his satchel.

"You mean, Crayon, like what Floru draws her portraits with for The Queen Mary?" asked Flounder with a puzzled look on his face.

"No. A Cranberry," said Toss as he threw one to Flounder and Ray. "Try it," Both Ray and Flounder looked nervous. They had

18

never eaten something so exotic before, much less the color red. "Do we just swallow it whole?" asked Ray.

"No, you simpleton, you chew it," said Toss. Both Ray and Flounder hesitantly placed the cranberry in their mouths and began to chew.

"Sour," said Ray.

"Tart," said Flounder.

"Exactly," said Toss.

"Smile and say, 'butter,'" Floru interrupted. "Now stay still for the next fifteen minutes while I make portraits of you," She got out her crayons to draw Toss, Ray, and Flounder sitting next to each in the pavilion.

"Butter," all three of them said while standing perfectly still.

"I never understood why we have to go through this," said Toss.

"It's for The Queen Mary. She likes to know what's going on in all of her friends lives," whispered Ray.

"I find it refreshing," said Flounder. Fifteen minutes passed and Toss pointed to a nearby picnicking table.

"Let's go sit at that picnicking table," said Toss. "I have more tale to tell."

Ray, Toss, and Flounder headed over to the picnicking table and sat down. "Imagine this. I'm taking my mid-morning siesta from converting. I awake and there standing in front of me is the most beautiful woman I've ever seen. Her eyes were brown like maple syrup. Her hair, was red like that cranberry you just ate. She stood nearly 6 feet tall, towering over me. Her hands soft and supple," said Toss.

"Just like The Queen Mary's hair?" asked Flounder.

"The very same. I was startled at first. I grabbed my dagger and threatened her by natural instinct. 'Stand back, Non-Believer,' I said. She merely smiled and winked."

"What did she smell like?" interrupted Ray.

"Raspberries," said Toss.

"'Raspberries'? What is a raspberry?"

19

"Ah Moses, I forgot you guys are simpletons. It's a type of fruit. It doesn't matter. She smelled amazing," continued Toss.

"I asked, 'Why did you wink at me?' She responded, 'Because my beliefs are not the same as you.' I couldn't believe my ears. How could someone so beautiful, so majestic, so peacock like not share my beliefs? How could this non-believer think differently? Now I could understand how simpletons, no offense, like you and Flounder, could possibly think differently. But her? It was an impossible thought. I stood there. Speechless. She was the woman of my dreams. She handed me a hanky with the initials B.O.O.B and left. I couldn't move. I couldn't speak. I was paralyzed with love."

"Nice to see you Toss. Kill any non-believers lately?" Mrs. Warwick yelled while walking past Toss, Ray, and Flounder.

"Lots. How is Professor Warwick?"

"Dead," said Mrs. Warwick.

"Sorry to hear that, it was nice seeing you," yelled Toss.

"Yeah," Mrs. Warwick said as she shook her head.

"What's her problem?" Toss asked as he watched Mrs. Warwick scurry down the street.

"She's angry about the rising prices on Peacock meat, I heard," said Ray.

"Yeah, something about the Dominades," said Flounder.

"Well, it's not my fault. Now what was I talking about?" said Toss.

"The amazing majestic woman you met," said Ray.

"Oh, that's right. The beauty. She grabbed my heart and never let go. I must find her. I must get back out there, beyond the city walls. I can't wait until my next tour of conversions. I must convert her. She must be mine," said Toss.

"Think she'll be easy to convert?" asked Flounder.

"You bet your shitty smelling feet," said Toss. "Any who. I got some shit to do, so you guys move along and get busy with your day. It was great catching up." The three embraced with a kiss on each other's ear as was accustom in Blueburrie and away they went.

Chapter Four

PRE-BALL

❧

"Giddy Yip," Mosh yelled as he steered his team of six small blue ponies on Fourth Avenue. Attached to the team of ponies was a large blue circus wagon, with Mosh sitting in the driver seat. As the wagon moved briskly down Fourth Avenue, the sound of bladder pipes bellowed. The smell of fresh cut flowers and roasted peacock filled the air. "Come on boys, Giddy Yip," Mosh yelled as he held a small broom on the left side of the wagon. As the team of ponies pulled the wagon throughout the street, Mosh swept back and forth to clean any peacock dung that was plastered to the street. "Giddy whoa," yelled Mosh, pulling on the reigns to slow the team and the wagon to a halt. He jumped out of the wagon with his juicer in hand, and quickly made his way to the back of the wagon. He opens the back door to reveal a freshly roasted peacock wrapped in iron foil. He lifted the foil, squirted juice, grabbed some flowers, and placed them on the side of the street. Mosh then threw his juicer into a bucket, grabbed his broom, and jumped back into the driver seat. "Giddy Yip. Giddy Yip," he yelled. He repeated the process down Fourth Avenue. "I just can't believe I have to do all this for the ball" he grumbled and blew in the bladder pipe.

"My body lies over the sea. My body lies over some apples. Now bring back my body, eat peas . . . ," Margarine sang as she carefully cleaned The Queen Mary's monocle collection. "I wonder if I'll ever own a monocle collection as vast as this Hornco," she said as she scratched behind her pet vole's ears. Hornco simply looked back at Margarine and shrugged.

"Oh, I know you're only a vole, but if I had one wish. I would wish you could turn into a Duke, and marry me someday. We could travel the world in search of beautiful monocles and I would hire a maiden to clean our collection for once. Just you and I, Hornco. Margarine and Hornco. Together. Forever," she whispered as Hornco looked up and shrugged again. "Oh Hornco, you're so indecisive."

"Margarine." The Queen Mary bellowed. "You better not be talking to that disgusting vole again."

"I wasn't," Margarine lied. She scurried up to The Queen Mary's bedroom.

"The odds of that rat--."

"Vole," Margarine interrupted.

"Vole," said The Queen Mary. "The odds of that Vole ever becoming a Duke are very slim. I know you've heard stories of creatures becoming human, but it's just not realistic. This isn't 2 B.C. It's the five-hundreds. Things like that just don't happen anymore."

"He's just my friend," Margarine said

"What? What did you say? He is NOT your friend," The Queen Mary commanded. "He is merely an acquaintance. How dare you say he's your friend? I am your friend. I am your only friend," The Queen Mary shouted.

"I'm sorry." Margarine said and began to cry.

"Sorry. You're sorry. You're a simpleton. You are nothing to me. I am royalty. My heart is divine. I have hundreds of friends. I live in a Castle. I eat Peacock ankles four times a week. My life is important. You're a simpleton," boasted The Queen Mary

"Yeah. You said that already," said Margarine.

"Well, I meant it. Now fetch my schmock. And my brush. And my hosiery. I need to get ready for the ball."

Down in the courtyard the dancing floor really started to present its true beauty. While Mosh finished up sweeping peacock dung, the band set up their instruments on the small stage surrounded in flowers. Near the center of the ballroom was a large iron foil wrapped peacock ready to be eaten. Tables surrounded the dance floor, draped in beautiful blue table clothes. "The guests will be arriving soon," Mosh said. "After cutting the flowers, decorating this venue, exercising Purk's bladder, picking up peacock shit, and juicing the peacock for the ball. I am exhausted. I deserve an ale," he gazed over at NumNuck's Tavern. "Maybe I have some time for just one before the ball." Mosh crossed Fourth Avenue. Just as he was about to enter NumNuck's, the door swung open. Out stumbled a very intoxicated and overly served Blur.

"Mush. Wish. Mish. Juice?" Blur mumbled at Mosh.

"What?" said Mosh.

"Wish. Do you mish wish and juice my cock?" Blur yells and points across the street at the Peacock wrapped in iron foil.

"Yeah. I juiced it. Thanks a lot, by the way. While you were pre-ballin' it, I ended up having to juice your peacock. Do you realize how much work I had to do today? Juicing the peacock just added to my ever-growing list of shit to do," yelled Mosh.

"Blurp. Did you over juice?" said Blur.

"'Over juice'? No. Thank the almighty that your nephew was there. He taught me exactly how much juice to use. Listen, That peacock better not have any mushy bones, that's all I have to say. Or it's going to be your ass. Your ass. Not mine. The Queen Mary isn't going to blame me for mushy bones in that bird," Mosh pushed Blur aside and walks into NumNuck's.

"I'll take another Ale," said Mrs. Warwick. NumNuck grabbed a glass from underneath the bar.

"Would you like any salt on that?" asked NumNuck.

"Just a tad on the rim," said Mrs. Warwick. "I like a nice salty ale." She winked as she looked to Ray and Flounder sitting at the bar.

"I once heard about a lake, as big as the eye could see, that was so salty, you could barely drink a gallon," Ray said.

"Salty Water?" said Mrs Warwick. "Who ever heard of such a thing?"

"It's true," said Ray. "My cousin, Toss. He's seen it with his very own eyes. Drank two gallons of it before he realized it was never going to quench his thirst."

"Oh. Toss. That one. The fancy Dominator cousin of yours. Peacock prices," as she grumbled and took a sip of her ale. "Mmm, salty."

"My cousin has seen such wild and amazing things. Have you ever left Blueburrie, Mrs. Warick?" Ray asked.

"Leave? Why would I leave?" she asked. "It's dangerous. There's nothing out there. We have everything we could ever want. If I want a salty ale, I can get it at NumNuck's Tavern. If I want fresh peacock wrists, I head over to Blur's Butcher. If I want to pet a peacock, I head to the park and pet one."

"I know. I just think there's so much more on the outside," Ray said.

"What do you want to die of Black Mold poisoning?" asked Mrs. Warwick.

"That sounds terrible. I'm probably allergic to black mold," said Flounder.

"We probably all are," yelled Ray. "All I'm saying is sometimes I wonder what it's like. What is it REALLY like beyond the city walls?"

"Well good luck trying to get a pass to the outside. The Queen Mary never lets anyone leave," Mrs. Warwick said.

"You know that my husband, the good Professor Warwick was studying facts about the outside world and he died. I still think it was because he was thinking about the outside world and the stress of it all killed him," said Mrs. Warwick.

"Smile and say, 'butter,'" Floru said.

"Highlight my cheekbones," said Mrs. Warwick.

"Already have the perfect shade of yellow," said Floru.

Ray, Flounder, and Mrs. Warwick all grouped together at the bar and yelled, "Butter."

"Where is Floru? I expect her to have some portraits for me," The Queen Mary asked while Margarine got started with the braids.

"I'm here, I'm here," shouted Floru quite out of breath from running up the stairs.

"Where are my portraits. I must have them. Give them to me now."

Floru handed The Queen Mary a fresh stack of recently painted portrait cards. "Lovely. Blueberry. Blueberry. Iron Foiled Peacock. I wonder if this is what's for dinner? Blueberry. A wonderful portrait of Mosh mopping up peacock pebbles. I surely hope Suzin isn't angry at Mosh for interfering with his job. A portrait of a live peacock looking at our roasted peacock, lovely. Oh, here's an interesting portrait. It's Mrs. Warwick, Ray, and Flounder. This portrait is very interesting. What were they doing? They seem to be having a good time without me. Floru, why wasn't I invited? Why didn't they want me to come? Did I say something to Ray to offend him? I just don't understand. I am divine. My hair is soft and supple. Why would they intentionally exclude me? This is unacceptable. I forbid them to meet at NumNuck's ever again. Call for my carriage. The blue one. With the blue wheels and the blue seats. I'm off to the ball," screamed The Queen Mary. "I must never be excluded."

Near the city center the crowd started to grow in anticipation of the official start of the ball. The band was practicing, the chefs were sharpening their knives, and the people were taking their seats. The sun was just about ready to set and there wasn't a cloud in the sky. Everything was going to be perfect for The Queen Mary's ball. Arriving backstage was Ray and Flounder fresh from a pre-ball ale from NumNuck's. "Oh my Almighty. I forgot my cummerbund," Ray told Flounder in a panic. "How can I tap dance without my cummerbund? Without it, I'll be off balance. I'm already nervous about my paradiddle. Now this. Flounder, what am I going to do?"

Flounder thought for a second. He didn't have any skills, and he certainly couldn't assist Ray with his paradiddle. "I've got it," he said. "Ray, take this," Flounder tore 5 inches off the bottom of his favorite shirt.

"Flounder, no. Your favorite shirt. Your mom gave you that shirt," cried Ray.

"No, Ray. It's perfect. You can use the bottom half of my shirt as a cummerbund. It'll look great. Flounder said. Flounder wrapped Ray's stomach with his homemade cummerbund and—with an exposed mid-drift—took a step back.

"You look great. Amazing. Dare I say, divine-ish," said Flounder.

"You're my best acquaintance. You really are. I don't know what I'd do without you," said Ray.

"Likewise," said Flounder.

Chapter Five

THE BALL

❧

The city center, now packed with The Queen Mary's friends came alive with her arrival. People cheered, whistled, and peacock called as The Queen Mary walked down a blue carpet. She waved with her nose held high. Stumbling behind her was Margarine, carrying the tail of The Queen Mary's beautiful dress and schmock. At the end of the blue carpet stood a ladder, nearly 150 feet high to a large platform. The Queen Mary grabbed the first rail as she proceeded to climb the ladder to her high perch above. People cheered and applauded as she climbed higher and higher. Finally, reaching the top, she walked over to the edge of the platform to address her friends. "My. . . Friends," began The Queen Mary, noticeably out of breath from her climb up the ladder. "My Closest Friends of Blueburrie. I welcome you to the XXVI'th ball. The day is great and we are safe. For my city walls protect us, today, tomorrow, and forever in the future. No one is allowed out, and few are allowed in, for your safety, your safety is my divine duty. For I am The Queen Mary. Royalty above the rest." People cheered, whistled, and peacock called.

"Now let us take 15 minutes for a moment of silence to remember all of my friends who have died in the last 15 years." The crowd came to a hush. All that could be heard was the occasional hiccup from Blur who had pre-balled it just a tad too much. "Now, let us say our Pledge of Allegiance to begin the opening ceremony for the ball," The Queen Mary said.

The crowd raised their hands high, like a peacock strutting, and began to chant. "We pledge allegiance, to the royal friend post, of the great city of Blueburrie. And to The Queen Mary, for which she stands, high up, on her platform, giving us protection and safety to all."

"That's satisfactory, simpletons. Let the ball begin," The Queen Mary bellowed. "Let's eat first. I can't wait for my lips to try some of that juicy peacock," she declared.

The carvers and servers appeared, as if out of thin air, and started to do their work. They open the iron foiled peacock to reveal a perfectly juiced bird.

"Perfection as always," Blur yelled out

"No thanks to me," grumbled Mosh under his breath. "Let's give 15 cheers for Blur. Our master butcher and peacock juicer," The Queen Mary commanded. "Hip, Hip, Hip, Hip, Hip, Hip. Hip, Hip, Hip, Hip, Hip, Hip, Hip, Hip, Hip, Hurray," the crowded cheered. Blur stumbled out on to the dance floor and took a bow.

"What an amazing party," Ray said, as he peeked behind the curtain.

"The peacock smells amazing," Flounder said.

"Go, eat, Flounder," Ray ordered.

"I couldn't. I'm too nervous and excited for you, Ray. I haven't eaten for two days, but that's okay. I can wait," Flounder said.

"The fact that you're starving and worry so for me, proves you are a great acquaintance," Ray said, kicking his foot into a paddle turn.

"Do you think you're ready?" asked Flounder.

"Ready as I'll ever be. I've done everything I can and with these tappers surely nothing can go wrong," Ray said.

"You guys ever think about joining the good fight to convert people to what we believe?" Toss asked as he sat at the kid's table. "You really should all think about it. When I was your age, I always wanted to tell people what to do. All of my acquaintances would listen to me because I was always right. All the kids looked up to me. I always got to pick the game we played, and I even got to make the rules. So, every time, I would win," Toss said as he took a bite of peacock smothered in gravy. "When you get older, you can join the Dominades like me. We get to do all sorts of cool things. See my helmet? It's made from an animal called an Elephant."

"Woah," the kids gasped in unison while Toss displayed his wares. "My boots. My boots are made from a dangerous animal called an alligator. It has sharp, shiny teeth and swims in the swamp."

"Did you wrestle the alligator yourself to get them?" asked one of the inquisitive children.

"No, I didn't. I took them clean off a dead non-believer's feet. That's the great thing about the Dominades. Whenever you see a dead non-believer, you can take their stuff."

"Woah," the kids gasped again.

"Think about it you tiny simpletons. Your life could be divine like mine," said Toss before walking away with a peacock bone between his teeth.

****

"Oh good. They're open," said Mrs. Warwick, noticing the light on in Blur's Butcher Shoppe.

"Hello Mrs. Warwick, you're out late. How can I help you?" said Hu as he stood behind the counter.

"Well, Hu, why aren't you at the ball? Don't you like balls?" asked Mrs. Warwick.

"Oh. I'd love to go. I wish I could. I've always wanted to go to a ball, but my uncle forces me to work. Mostly twenty hours a day. I barely have any time to do anything for myself," said Hu.

"Oh, that's terrible. When do you sleep?" asked Mrs. Warwick.

"Well, mostly standing up behind the counter when no one is here. I know I shouldn't but I just can't help myself. It's almost as if my body needs sleep," said Hu. "Sometimes I just wonder if this is the right job for me. My uncle says it is but I sometimes ponder what's on the outside of the city walls. Maybe there's more for me? Maybe I could start my own shop and settle down with a nice girl. I sometimes wonder, maybe that girl will have a sister and that sister will have a son. Then I could be an uncle just like my uncle Blur. Then, and maybe I'm kidding myself, but maybe I could start a butcher shop of my own and force my nephew to work long hours. It's probably all just peacock-wash," said Hu.

"It certainly sounds like just that," Mrs. Warwick scolded. "Hu, it's dangerous. The outside world is full of danger and mold. People die every day just walking around."

"I suppose that's true. I guess I'm just dreaming," said Hu. "Now what can I help you with?"

"Well, I'm baking a peacock quiche at home and I need one more peacock egg," said Mrs. Warwick.

"Great. We have this new wooden sign order system we just added this afternoon. It's much easier and you won't have to rely on me for messing up your order," said Hu.

"Oh. Well. How does it work?" asked Mrs. Warwick as she gazed at the wooden tablet on the counter.

"Very easy. You see that piece of bark that says 'New Open Order'? Press that bark."

"'New Open Order' got it," said Mrs. Warwick.

"Great. Now press Cold Pantry and then press Peacock Accessories."

"What?"

"Ok, Press Cold Pantry," said Hu.

"Ok, Pantry," repeated Mrs Warwick.

"No, press Cold Pantry," said Hu.

"I did."

"No you pressed Pantry. Press Cold Pantry," said Hu.

"Oh. I see. Cold Pantries."

"No, not Cold Pantries. That's if you have multiple pantries at your house," said Hu.

"I only have one pantry," said Mrs. Warwick.

"Yeah, that's fine. I just need you to press Cold Pantry."

"Oh. Ok, Cold Pantry," said Mrs. Warwick.

"Perfect. Now you'll want to press Peacock Accessories. It should be the only button you can press."

"Yes, but I want an egg. I don't need to accessorize any peacocks," said Mrs. Warwick.

"I know. It's just how the tablet is set up. I'll need you to press Peacock Accessories," said Hu.

"Ok. But I think you're wrong," said Mrs. Warwick.

"Ok, I pressed it. The tablet is blank. It doesn't say anything now," said Mrs. Warwick.

"It should say Egg Like Items," said Hu.

"Nope. It doesn't say anything. It's just blank. Nothing. Oh. Wait. It's says Error in Open Order press yes to start over or no to continue. Should I press, yes?" asked Mrs. Warwick before proceeding to press yes.

"No. Don't press yes."

"Too late," said Mrs. Warwick. "

Never mind," said Hu. "Let me just get your eggs."

"Egg," Mrs. Warwick corrected him.

"Egg. That's right," sighed Hu.

Back at the ball, things were really starting to happen. Floru sat in the corner feverishly drawing portrait cards. People dancing, singing, eating peacock, and having an amazing time. The Queen Mary sat high up on her platform watching her friends below. "They are having such a wonderful time. They are truly blessed to have me as their Queen Mary. Divine, holy, and special. That's probably what most of them are saying about me right now."

"I am having so much fun, watching other people have fun," Margarine said as she watched the people nearly 150 feet below her.

"You may be a simpleton like the rest of them," said The Queen Mary. "But you certainly know how to spot people having fun. When do you suppose Ray will start his dancing. I hope he saves it for the big finale. I heard his tappers so I know he's here. Summon my new friends. I want them to meet me," said The Queen Mary.

Margarine wrote a tiny note and attached it to a blue jay's leg. "To Mosh. The Queen would like to summon her new friends, Gimlett and Morehouse." She set the bird free as it flew straight into the air. It flew towards the Castle and back down along Fourth Avenue. It then flew straight up in the air again and silhouetted against the full moon now presenting itself. The blue jay came swooping back down towards the city center and landed directly on Mosh's shoulder.

"Ah, a new Jay," said Mosh, referring to the message attached to the tiny leg of the blue jay. "It appears The Queen Mary would like us to summon Gimlett and Morehouse. Guards. bring them in. Single file please. Directly this way. Post Haste," Mosh commanded as two massive guards left the city center, swords in hand.

"Make way. Make way. The Queen Mary's new friends have arrived," yelled the Guards as they push their wheelbarrows through the crowd. Sitting up straight in the wheelbarrows were the two six-month olds, Gimlett and Morehouse. Their eyes as yellow as the sun, and as cute as possible.

"Stop the music. Stop the dancing. Stop the prancing and singing. Stop eating and drinking and talking and if anyone is stalking. Stop that too. My new friends have arrived and I have something important to say," yelled the Queen Mary.

The music stopped abruptly mid-song and people froze in place on the dancefloor. Some of The Queen Mary's friends still chewing with food in their mouths, simply swallowed pieces of peacock whole. Others who happened to be taking a sip of ale, froze, with cups still pressed against their lips. The Queen Mary's friends knew that when she spoke you did best to listen.

"My friends. I want to introduce you to my new friends, Gimlett and Morehouse. They are some of the best friends I think I'll ever meet. They are six months old and have tiny hands. They are small and they are simple, but they are wonderful. They don't know how to speak, yet. But I know with time they will start to form words using their mouths. With time they will walk. And more importantly, with time they will learn to obey. For I am The Queen Mary. Ruler of all of Blueburrie. Divine. Keeping everyone safe. I am royalty. And you. You my friends of Blueburrie are mere simpletons. With that. . .," The Queen Mary paused. "I'd like to present, one of my favorite friends, Ray. To show off his tapping feet. Ray. Dance. Dance now. Start the music and dance," The Queen Mary commanded.

"Break a Coccyx," whispers Flounder as he gives Ray a quick hug. Ray runs to the middle of the stage and takes a bow. The crowd cheers and all eyes are upon him. The music starts, the dancing begins. It's Ray's turn to tap his way to huge applause.

"Tappers, don't fail me now," Ray said aloud to himself. He started slow and began to drawback, flipped into a flap heel turn, and finished off with a hop shuffle.

The Queen Mary yelled out, "Dance Faster."

Ray tapped faster, and brought out his "three b's" The Back Essence, the Bombershay, and Buffalo. His tappers sparked on the dance floor below him.

The Queen Mary bellowed out, "Better. Dance better."

Ray, now sweating, was in a frenzy of Dig Toes, Maxie Fords, and Paddle Turns.

"Dance longer," The Queen Mary yelled. Ray, realizing that he was out of moves, began to paradiddle over and over to appease The Queen Mary's request to dance longer. Despite dancing for nearly 15 minutes, Ray simply couldn't keep up. He fell to his knees and looked up at The Queen Mary.

She looked back at Ray with utter disgust. "Guards. Get him off my stage. Take him to the Dungeon," The Queen Mary screamed. His feet bloodied with blisters, Ray stood as the Guards grabbed him.

Flounder yelled out, "Ray. Wait," and ran towards the guards. "I'm coming too. Ray and I are acquaintances,".

"Whatever," said The Queen Mary. "Take them away."

"Both of them?" asked the guard.

"Yes. Ray and Flounder."

"These guys?" asked the Guard

"Yes. Those simpletons on stage. Both of them. Ray and Flounder," screamed The Queen Mary.

"Your command is our doing, and our doing is your command," said the Guard. They grabbed Flounder and Ray and escorted them off the stage to a nearby prisoner wagon. "Get in," they said.

The Queen Mary turned to the crowd of friends. "You see my friends of Blueburrie. This is what happens. This is what happens when you aren't practicing and you associate with others without me," The Queen Mary spoke assuredly. "When you have fun, and cock about with others when I'm not there everything suffers. Everyone suffers. Ray decided to waste time today at NumNucks, chatting with **my** friends. Look what it's brought me. Look what he's brought us. His dance moves suffered. And we all suffered for it. The ball is ruined. It was all a waste of time. Ray ruined it for everyone. I'm leaving," The Queen Mary said as she started to climb down her ladder. People began to shuffle off, single file. Silence fell upon the crowd as they walk back to their homes.

Chapter Six

THE QUEEN MARY, THE COG

"Throw a cast on the mast and heave ho," Captain Limb shouted as he walked to his over-sized steering wheel.

"Did you have a nice nap?" asked First Lieutenant.

"It was divine. Truly divine," said Captain Limb. "What a glorious day to be at sea. The Queen Mary, the Cog is in top form today. We are sailing directly wind-side and all anchors are up. Yes, this day will be great. It surely will," the Captain declared.

Nearly 28 meters in length The Queen Mary, the Cog was an impressive sight. She had just celebrated her six-month birthday as a Cog, which was the newest technology in ship making at the time. The hull was made of a timber that was harvested from the tallest spruce trees. The glue that held the decking together was mixed with blueberries and peacock dung to give the essence of blue. At the bow was a sculpture of a beautiful peacock being ridden by The Queen Mary herself, for whom the ship was named. The Queen Mary, the Cog held a crew of nearly forty souls and in charge of her stood a four-foot six burly man named Captain Limb.

"Captain, we are heading upwind. If we turn around, we'll be traveling downwind. Do you confirm?" asked First Lieutenant.

"That does sound about right," said Captain Limb. "But I'll want another opinion if you don't mind."

"Of course," said First Lieutenant.

"Four Bells and Mark Twain," yelled a deck officer near the bow of the ship.

"Very well. Keep me posted of any changes in twain or bells," said Captain Limb. Even though it was early in the morning the ship was alive as they sailed westward. The seas were calm, but Captain Limb had a funny feeling in his stomach. He certainly was no stranger to sea sickness. It often would take quite a bit of time for the captain to get his sea legs.

"It's been nearly four weeks. The sea sickness still with you Captain?" asked First Lieutenant.

"It'll be fine. Maybe if I take another nap. Sometimes these things just take time. I just get so dizzy and sick to my stomach when I sail," said Captain Limb.

"Have you tried any of those blueberry motion sickness pills?" asked the First Lieutenant.

"I did. Maybe I should try more. I only had a box," said Captain Limb.

"Four Bells past the mark," yelled a deckhand.

"Very well," said the Captain. "I'm going down for a nap. Wake me in three hours."

"Yes Sir," said the First Lieutenant.

"Deckhand Dunky, what is our current heading?" asked First Lieutenant.

"Westward. We're heading west with nothing but open sea and Pottstown in sight," said Dunky.

"Well. It's about time we started thinking about turning around. Pottstown lies on the edge of the world. We'd hate to fall off the side of earth wouldn't we?" said First Lieutenant.

"What if we kept going?" asked Dunky.

"Kept going? What on earth do you mean? If we kept going, we'd obviously fall off the side of the world," said First Lieutenant. "Oh Dunky. This is why you're a deckhand and I'm a First Lieutenant," said First Lieutenant.

"I know sir. I've just been thinking, lately. It doesn't seem right. Wouldn't all the water just fall off the side of the earth if it was flat? How come me sees water for miles and not space? Most things in life are round or spherical. Something just doesn't add up," said Dunky.

"Listen, Dunky you're one of the best deckhands on this Cog. You're so creative and always come up with great inventions. Remember your idea about how well pitchforks work and you made a smaller tiny version that we called pitches to eat with? You rounded all our spoons, instead of flattening them. That gave us all the ability to eat soup. But Dunky Columbus, this idea of yours that the earth isn't flat. It's all pigwash," said First Lieutenant.

"I know sir. I just thought."

"Well stop thinking. Spend your time thinking about something else. The earth is flat. Scientists have proven it. And for Almighty's sake, even the The Queen Mary herself agrees the earth is as flat as the bottoms of your feet," said First Lieutenant.

"Aye, aye, First Lieutenant. I'll go ahead and steer us round. Now heading straight east. Eastward ho," Dunky said as The Queen Mary, the Cog's sails shifted and turned now heading straight east.

"Well, you really did a number on this finger. I've never seen something so bruised before," said Dr. Dunston.

"Me was trying to lift a jig and me got it caught in between the gimbal and the fort knot," said Deckhand 919.

"I have no idea what the hell you just said, but it sounds like it hurt. Do you think you broke it?" asked Dr Dunston.

"The fort knot? Well, you can't really break rope," said the deckhand.

"No, the finger. The finger, do you think you broke the finger?" yelled Dr Dunston.

"Me not sure. Me guess so?" said the deckhand as he grimaced in slight pain.

"Well. You're wrong. I don't think you broke your finger. As I see it we have a few options. One, I could amputate the finger. This would remove your finger and we wouldn't have to guess on whether it's broken. Two, we can dip your finger in hot wax and cause you more pain. Three, and I believe this is the best option by the way, you can try my personal elixir medicine known as Finger-Aise. It's a cream you rub on your chest, four times a day. It will cause a painful rash, but it should remove the pain you feel in your finger," said Dr. Dunston.

"Me needs me fingers. Me'd rather deal with the rash," said the deckhand.

"Consider it done. Here's the first week supply of my Finger-Aise cream. I'll talk with Captain Limb about docking your pay for the medicine payments," said Dr. Dunston.

"Aye, aye," said the deckhand as he headed up to the forward aft deck.

"Another job done," said Dr. Dunston as he took off his examination spectacles and placed them on his medical desk.

Above deck near the stern, a group of deckhands crowded around First Lieutenant for a whaling lesson. "Now. When I throw the harpoon, you want to make sure you don't tighten your wrist. If you let your wrist go silly, you'll add a nice twist to the harpoon as it cascades through the air and in to the flesh of a majestic blue whale," said First Lieutenant.

"Me's right-handed, does that matter?" asked one of the deckhands.

"It doesn't. As long as you keep either your left or your right wrist silly, you should be able to give it that old English we're looking for."

"Me's not English," said one of the deckhands.

"Doesn't matter. This is all about the silliness in your wrist. Keep it silly, and you'll kill your willy. Is what I always say. And before any of you ask, I'm referring to a whale when I say willy. Does everyone understand? "

"Aye, aye," the deckhands yelled out.

As The Queen Mary, the Cog sailed to the east, a sharp eastern wind caught the sails, making them flutter. "What was that?" asked the captain as he popped out of his bed. That seemed like a flutter. I wonder if the wind has picked up? he thought to himself. Never mind, I suppose. If any danger would present itself surely my First Lieutenant would report it. Now where's my journal? He reached to his bed table for his journal, opened it and started writing. *It's been nearly four weeks and we've been sailing for most of it. Well, I mean, it's not that we're not sailing. I mean, I've been using the sails for the most of journey. A few days back, I had to ask some of the deckhands to row. Most of them are simpletons and didn't grasp the concept, but we managed to do some pretty exciting 360s and that was a good laugh. Despite not having most of the wind at our backs, I feel my quest to kill a blue whale for The Queen Mary is fleeting. We haven't seen any signs of whales in weeks and my instinct tells me that we will fail. My instinct is generally hit or miss, but this time, I feel like it's a hit. I feel we will never accomplish our goal of slaughtering a majestic blue whale in time for The Queen Mary's birthday. Oh how I wish to please that majestic, divine woman.* The captain set down his feather pen and looked out the window.

"Fire at Will," First Lieutenant commanded as several deckhands took aim. Out nearly five hundred and twenty-eight yards stood Chef Will on top of the ships only dingy.

"You slimy bastards. I'm going to spit in your stew and fart in your sweet bread," Chef Will yelled.

"Me's going to hit him first," said one of the deckhands.

"No, you won't. Me's will," said another as he took careful aim. The roar of the cannons fired as cannonballs splashed all around Chef Will.

"You heartless, snail eating, muffin bastard asses," yelled Chef Will.

"Oh, how I love Chef Will's insults," said Captain Limb as he joined First Lieutenant on the fire bridge.

"I am also very fond. I think it was a great idea to start taking target practice at him after hearing him down in the galley after a few dinner services," said First Lieutenant.

"I agree," said Captain Limb. "He definitely has quite the tongue for a great insult. It really riles up the boys," Captain Limb said as he chuckled. "Fire fast, and fire up. Keep those cannons pointed outward and forward aft. Let him have it," yelled the Captain as the cannons roared with explosions.

"Cease Fire, cease fire and pull Chef Will in," yelled Captain Limb.

"Now we got close, but we still need more practice," said First Lieutenant. As the deckhands pulled the tether that was attached to the ship's only dingy with Chef Will, shaken from fear.

"You bloody peacocks. I'll never understand why you use your only chef on board as target practice. Don't be surprised if your oyster Rockefellers are a little extra salty tonight. You bloody sons of peahens," grumbled Chef Will. The crew laughed and pointed at his soiled pants as he climbed back aboard.

"Me's thinks he shat himself," one yelled.

"Me's agree," said another deckhand.

"Oh Ha Ha, go ahead laugh you morons. Go ahead and laugh. You'll all be sorry," yelled Chef Will.

"I'll be down in my cabin, I'm feeling a little off," said Captain Limb as he walked slowly away from First Lieutenant.

"I hope you feel better," he said. The captain, still feeling a little dizzy from being topside, sat at his writing desk and grabbed his journal. *Log entry number XXXIVX. Still feeling a bit sick. The seas are calm this afternoon, but I still can't get used to being topside. I suspect I'll need to take another nap to get more wear on my sea legs. We got the boys all excited and broke out the cannons for a little target practice. Chef Will was angry, as usual. He just doesn't understand the morale boost it brings the crew by shooting seven-pound cannonballs at him. I suspect I'll need to have First Lieutenant have a talk with him. Still no sign of any whales or whale like activity. The stress of not having any whale meat on board is beginning to affect my soul. I fear we will never catch and kill that blue beast to appease The Queen Mary.*

The sun set as Captain Limb gazed out his port hole window. Another day had passed, and no whale. The Queen Mary, the Cog was sailing further and further into the wild blue ocean hoping to find that elusive blue whale. Tomorrow would be another day.

"Nine casts past the port rudder," called out one of the deckhands as he rang the ship's bell.

"It feels like me chest is on fire," said "Deckhand 919" as he scratched and itched his chest.

"Well. Let's take a look," said Dr. Dunston. "Have you been applying my special creme, Finger-Aise like I prescribed?"

"Me surely am. Three times a day. But me chest is as scratchy as a willow pad," said deckhand.

"Well. Let's see. How does your finger feel?" asked Doctor Dunston.

"Me finger feels great, but my chest. My chest," yelled the deckhand.

"Yeah. Finger-Aise has been known to give unacceptable rashes. There is a cure. I have a pill you will need to take that will cure that rash. It's fairly large and often gets stuck in people's throat, but I feel it's your best bet to combat that rash."

"Me'll try anything," said the deckhand.

"Ok. Besides the occasional pill choking, you may or may not notice some weakness in your knees and elbows," said Doctor Dunston.

"Me don't care. Me rarely uses those, me thinks," said the deckhand.

"In that case, this pill will be perfect. I'll let the captain know to deduct the cost from your pay," said Doctor Dunston.

As the sun rose over the bow of The Queen Mary, the Cog, not a raincloud was in the sky. The early morning crew of deckhands were polishing the brass and scrubbing the decks in preparation for the day of whale hunting.

"Dead whales love a clean deck," laughed First Lieutenant.

"Good morning, Deckhands. Keep up the good work."

"Aye, aye, First Lieutenant. Sir. A new jay is flying in," said the deckhand. A beautiful blue jay flew majestically a few feet above the water line. Swooping up at the last minute, it flew straight at First Lieutenant and landed perfectly on his arm.

"Lovely," said First Lieutenant, as he ripped the jay message off. The blue jay squawked in slight pain and flew away. *To Captain Limb - From The Queen Mary. My dearest captain. It has come to my attention that you have been whale hunting for quite some time. I find it very admirable of you for trying to catch and kill a blue whale all in my honor. But, I need for your ship to pick up a supply of blueberry jam located in the port of Pottstown immediately. My supply of jam is dangerously low and I feel that the winter may bring a shortage. Please direct your ship and crew in the direction of Pottstown, and retrieve my jam with the utmost urgency."*

Captain Limb isn't going to be too keen on this idea, thought First Lieutenant. He knew the captain hated change or any precarious situations. Once the Captain awoke things might be a little tense. It was 9:30am and he decided to wait until the Captain awoke at the normal time of 10:00am.

"Ten bells and forty-four whistles," yelled one of the deckhands.

"Main Jib is Aft," yelled another deckhand as he tied a sailor's knot in a random string hanging from the railing. The captain appeared from down below the main deck and walked over to First Lieutenant.

"What a wonderful morning this is," he said as he took a sip of hot blueberry tea.

"It surely is. How are you feeling this morning?" asked First Lieutenant.

"I'm feeling okay. I'm still pretty dizzy and my stomach is quite a bit nauseous, but overall I feel better than I did yesterday," said the Captain.

"That's wonderful to hear," said First Lieutenant

"What's the news of this morning? How's the crew? How's the ship?" asked the captain.

"Well, the ship is in wonderful condition. The jibs are aft, as you may have heard. The rudder seems to be functioning properly. We have a fresh coat of blueberry lacquer on the main deck. All the ropes that are dangling have been put in to sailors' knots. We even greased the captain's wheel and we removed the squeak from most of the deckhand's boots. Any squeaky boots that still remained we simply threw overboard, because we know how you hate the sound of squeaky boots," said First Lieutenant.

"Wonderful to hear. I despise the sound. Much prefer tapping. And how's the crew this morning?" asked the Captain.

"Wonderful as well. Well, some have been complaining about a chest rash that seems to be working its way around the boat, but I'm sure it's perfectly manageable. Dr. Dunston more than likely has a cure," said First Lieutenant.

"Ah, yes, Doctor Dunston. You know he cured my shingles and my scurvy several years ago. The man is a saint. He always has the best solution in mind. Very talented Doctor, I would say. The very best. I'm glad to hear the crew is functioning so well. And any other news?" asked the Captain.

"Well. Here's the thing," said First Lieutenant.

"Thing?" the captain asked as he set down his blueberry tea.

"Yeah. Well the thing is. A new jay arrived this morning from The Queen Mary."

"The Queen Mary herself?" asked the Captain.

"The very same. You see, the thing is, she's requested that we change course and head to Pottstown," said First Lieutenant.

"Pottstown? Why? We're currently heading directly away from Pottstown, aren't we?" asked the Captain.

"Yes. Very good Captain. We are in fact, sailing away from Pottstown this very moment. The thing is, she'd like us to head back to Pottstown and retrieve a shipment of blueberry jam. "

"Blueberry Jam? But we're supposed to be hunting for whales. How can we hunt whales if our course is set for retrieving jam?" the captain said as panic started to set in his voice.

"Well, Sir, I'm sure we can still hunt whales."

"Along the way? You suppose we can hunt whales along the way. Well, First Lieutenant it's simply not that easy. Our deckhands have never been trained to hunt whales and sail to retrieve blueberry jam before. No one will know what to do. We don't have the proper tools in place. Does anyone know how to store jam? What temperature does jam need to be stored? How often do we need to turn the bottles? Do we even need to turn the bottles?" the captain said as he began to pace back and forth in a panic.

"Sir, I'm sure. . . ."

"You're sure of what? You're sure everything will be fine? It won't be fine. We simply need to rethink this. Have the deckhands all untie the sailor's knots immediately. We can't sail with those tied," demanded Captain Limb.

"But, sir."

"No buts, First Lieutenant. You agree that although I am not feeling very well, that I am still in charge, don't you?" asked the captain.

"I agree Captain. Untie the knots," First Lieutenant yelled.

"Give me the jay, I must read this myself," demanded the captain as he grabbed it from First Lieutenant's hand. "I must study this and read it over in my quarters. Join me after the knots have been successfully untied," the captain ordered as he walked down the stairs.

"*But, I need for your ship to pick up a supply of blueberry jam located in the port of Pottstown immediately,*" the captain read the jay out loud. "Immediately. Immediately. What could The Queen Mary possibly mean? Immediately?" the captain said as he read the jay and paced back and forth. "This just doesn't add up. Blueberry Jam? Pottstown? Jam. Pottstown. Immediately," he started to say over and over. He sat in his captain's chair and began to rub his temples. I feel sicker than ever. We need to get back to Pottstown. And we have to do it immediately. I wonder what direction we're travelling now the captain thought to himself. "First Lieutenant," the captain yelled.

"Just untie the knots," First Lieutenant said to one of the deckhands.

"But me just got done tying it," said the Deckhand.

"I know, but we need to untie them. Captain's orders."

"Sir, the captain is calling for you. Me was walking past his quarters and he started yelling for you," said the Deckhand.

"Oh great. Now what does he want?" said First Lieutenant.

"Alright boys I need you to untie all these sailor's knots as fast as you can. Anywhere you see a knot, check and see if it's tied in a sailor like fashion, and untie the damn thing. Captain's orders."

"Aye, aye," said the deckhands.

"Sir, you wanted to see me?" asked First Lieutenant.

"Yes, yes. I wanted to see you. I called for you nearly two minutes ago. Almighty, I feel sick. So dizzy. Anyway. I was reading The Queen Mary's jay. She says immediately. What direction are we currently heading in?" asked the Captain.

"Currently, well currently we're heading east, away from Pottstown," said First Lieutenant.

"Away from Pottstown. Away from Pottstown. Immediately. This is quite the challenge. We're currently sailing away from Pottstown and we need to be sailing towards Pottstown. How quickly could we turn around?" asked Captain Limb.

"Immediately," said First Lieutenant. "Immediately. There's that word again. I simply don't understand. Let's continue on course for now until I can think clearer. I feel so sick, even my blueberry tea hasn't settled my stomach. I'm going to take a nap. Please go above deck and make sure no deckhands have any squeaky shoes, and also that all the sailor's knots have been untied," said the captain.

"Yes Sir," said First Lieutenant.

"Whale ho," screamed the deckhand. A majestic blue whale breached the water ahead and came crashing down into the sea.

The first lieutenant shushed the deckhand. "The Captain is napping. We must be completely silent," he scolded as he ran to the bow to see the whale.

"Me thinks he's a seventy-footer," said the deckhand as he whispered to First Lieutenant.

"Seventy-five," he corrected him as he looked through his looking glass. "Nasty one too. You see how he's flapping his tail and jumping out of the water? He's warning us. Stay away or he'll swallow us whole. These creatures are not to be toyed with. They are dangerous, vicious animals looking to dominate the earth with their sheer size alone. If you look closely, you can see his eyes. His eyes are full of hate and anger," the first lieutenant said.

"Should me get me harpoon?" the deckhand asked.

"Keep your side arm harpoon at the ready. You never know if this bastard will charge. Unfortunately, we must let this one be. The captain has given strict orders on letting him nap while he figures out what type of solution we need to get The Queen Mary's jam," said First Lieutenant.

As the whale breached the sea again, he stuck his tail high out of the water and waved as The Queen Mary, the Cog went by. "You see. He's trying to taunt us. He's trying to wave us in to eat us,." the first lieutenant said. "These beasts are only good for two thing: Oil lamps and Tube Steak. The almighty only created them for that purpose, and that purpose only."

"Evil, nasty creatures," the deckhand said as he stowed his harpoon in his side holster.

"Evil, nasty creatures indeed. I once heard a tale of a man who took his family out bluegill fishing one evening. He and his family were minding their own business, catching and killing bluegills when a terrifying blue whale started to scream at them. Making all these horrible moaning noises and waving its tail like a maniac. The father stood up and told the whale that he wasn't 'interested in any horseplay.' But do you think the whale listened? He certainly did not. The whale just kept getting closer and closer. Finally, the father stood up and yelled, 'Promptly remove yourself from this district..'

"Did the whale listen?" asked the deckhand.

"Nope. It was as if the whale had no clue what a district even was. He just kept getting closer and closer. Moaning and groaning and spraying what can only be assumed as acid from its huge hole in the top of its head. The family panicked and started to scream. 'Almighty help us. Help us from this moronic beast.' It was all for not. For the whale was evil, like all whales are. The whale swam right underneath the family's innocent fishing boat and breached the water, just like it's been doing here, and swallowed them whole. The whole family. Whole swallowed. The beast groaned and moaned and swam to the deep," First Lieutenant said.

"What happened to the family?" asked the deckhand. "The family? Like I just said they were whole swallowed. By the whale. Never to be seen again. Some say they are still living in that beast of a moronic whale. I think there could be some truth to that," said First Lieutenant.

"Do you think that could ever happen to us?" said the deckhand.

"Probably. Possibly. Most Definitely," said First Lieutenant. "I certainly wouldn't bet against it. Whales are the most revenge seeking creatures on the planet."

Several hours passed and the sun began to set over the horizon. The winds were gusty all afternoon which gave The Queen Mary, the Cog, a considerable spike on their daily average of sixty miles per day. Down below deck Chef Will was busy preparing the night's supper. "Me's wondering what's for dinner?" asked one of the deckhands.

"Chicken," joked the chef.

"Chicken? What's chicken?" asked the deckhand with a puzzled look on his face.

"I was just kidding. We'll be having Clams Casino for dinner," said the chef.

"Aye. Not again," said the deckhand. "Can't we get some bluegills or peacock every once and while? Me's get sick of shellfish all the time," said the deckhand.

"I swear to the almighty. All you deckhands do is complain. The shrimp scampi is too dry. My peacock wellington has burnt edges. My blueberry Kringle is stale. I'm getting really sick and tired of all the jokes and constant ridicule. I'm only human. I can only take so much before I'm going to explode," yelled Chef Will.

"Explode like your soufflés?" laughed the deckhand. Chef Will just glared at the deckhand as he cracked a clam open and drained the juices.

"Yeah. Just like my soufflés," Chef Will said while gritting his teeth.

"Any news to report before I go down for the night?" asked First Lieutenant to one of his deckhands.

"Nothing to report, sir. Still heading east. The wind is strong. We're making some great headway," said the deckhand as he pointed to the sails being completely full of wind.

"Head way in the wrong direction," grumbled First Lieutenant. "The captain is still asleep I assume?" asked the deckhand.

"Yes. He's out like a baby peachick," said the First Lieutenant.

"I hate to wake him. Poor guy slept right through dinner service. You know he hasn't been feeling too well."

"Me know, his sea legs," said the deckhand.

"Yeah, he hasn't quite got them yet. Sometimes it takes time. Well, at any rate, I'm off to bed. Please wake me in the morning and stay on this course. We'll see what the captain wants to do once he awakes,"

"Six bells past the mark. Twain Sixty phantoms and course forward," yelled the deckhand as the sun started to rise over the horizon. The winds were strong this morning as The Queen Mary, the Cog, pushed through the massive waves on her easterly course. First Lieutenant walked up the steps from below deck and rubbed the sleep out of his eyes.

"Good morning First Lieutenant. How did you sleep?"

"Divine-ish. Simply Divine-ish" said First Lieutenant.

"What's our course this morning?"

"Straight East. As east as east can be. Just like you said. Keep going east, that's what you said last night. Straight east. Right?" asked the deckhand.

"Straight east, I did say that" said First Lieutenant.

"Has Captain Limb awoken yet?" asked First Lieutenant.

"Not that I'm aware. I did see him last night doing his normal sleep walking around the upper deck, but nothing out of the ordinary," said the deckhand.

"He does get dangerously close to the edge of the ship when he does that, but at least he's getting some rest," said First Lieutenant.

"Who is dangerous?" asked Captain Limb as he came up from his quarters.

"We were just talking about you. I was just commenting on how you like to sleepwalk around the deck late at night. It can get pretty dangerous when you're up on that cat walk," said First Lieutenant.

"I don't sleep walk. I mean, I know I like to take the occasional stroll when I'm tired, but me? Sleepwalk? No. Never," said Captain Limb. First Lieutenant and the deckhand just gave each other a look and went about doing their business.

"So. What's the news of this morning? How is the crew? How is the ship?" asked the captain.

"Wonderful. The crew is pretty full after Clams Casino last night. I heard a lot of people saying that the clams were a little clammy tasting, but I didn't think so. Some of the guys bit down on some clam shells, but I don't think any one was seriously injured. If so, I'm sure they'll see Dr. Dunston," said First Lieutenant.

"Very well. Sorry I missed dinner last night. My stomach. My stomach is still a little queasy because of these damn rough seas. Speaking of, how is the ship performing this morning?" asked the captain.

"In great shape. She's at the top of her game. Heading east and making great progress," said First Lieutenant.

"Wonderful. Perfect. I love when we make great progress. And is there any news this morning?" asked the captain.

"Well. No news today, but we still have that jay we got from The Queen Mary yesterday about the jam," said First Lieutenant.

"What jam? The Queen Mary is in a jam?" asked Captain Limb.

"No, her jam. Her blueberry jam."

"Blueberry Jam?" asked the captain.

"Yes, the blueberry jam she wanted us to pick up in Pottstown. Don't you remember?" asked First Lieutenant.

"Of course, I remember. Well, are we making great progress towards Pottstown?" asked the captain.

"We're heading away from Pottstown. Remember? Yesterday you told me that you were going to come up with a solution, and you wanted to sleep on it."

"Of course, I remember," yelled Captain Limb. "I told you I'd come up with a solution, and I have one. We should have turned around yesterday. We're clearly heading in the wrong direction. Would you confirm?" asked the captain.

"Oh definitely. I can confirm," said First Lieutenant.

"We have a real problem here. The wind is pretty strong today," said the captain.

"It was even stronger yesterday. We made nearly 28 knots," said First Lieutenant.

"I certainly applaud the speed efforts. I mean that's great speed. but we're going in the wrong direction. Pottstown is to the west, and we're currently travelling east. Have been for nearly two days. The Queen Mary has said that she'd like us to head to Pottstown immediately. I'm still a little unclear what she means, but I know that we have a major problem in that we're heading east," said the captain.

"I totally agree. The easiest solution would be to just turn the ship around."

"But is the easy solution always the right solution?" Captain Limb interrupted.

"Well. No, but. . ." said First Lieutenant.

"Again, with the buts. First Lieutenant, we have been acquaintances for over fourteen years. I have constant faith in your decisions. I get thrills and chills questioning every one of them. Yet, for the life of me, you insist on causing me to have diarrhea. The stress of your decisions and suggestions and constant badgering makes me ill with fever rashes. I understand the predicament we are in, but I simply can't agree with your assessment. I must retreat to my quarters. I must come up with a solution for this complicated problem that doesn't have an easy solution, despite what you might think." The captain turned, pointed at First Lieutenant and left.

"Shall we continue eastward?" asked one of the deckhands.

"Yes, continue on," sighed First Lieutenant.

"Me can't swallow me pill because me chipped me tooth on a clam shell," said the deckhand as he hopped up on Dr Duston's examination table.

"Chef Will serving clams again, is he?" asked the doctor as he grabbed a candle to get a better look.

"Open wide and say 'Ha.'"

"Like me laughing?" asked the deckhand.

"No, say just the first part. 'Ha' and open wide," said the doctor.

"Me Arse?" the deckhand said as he went to grab his butt cheeks with a puzzled look on his face.

"No. No, not your ass. Your mouth. Open your mouth wide and say 'Ha.' Not haha, just ha," said the doctor. "Yes, it appears you chipped your tooth pretty bad here. You've got some significant enamel erosion on your maxillary teeth."

"Me What?" asked the deckhand.

"Your maxillary teeth. I also see something that concerns me here. The amount of plaque is causing a periodontal abscess. If we don't do something about this now, you're definitely going to pay more for it later," said the Doctor as he grabbed a cotton swab from the jar.

"How much is this going to cost I?" asked the deckhand.

"Significant amounts. But not nearly as much as you'd have to pay later if you wait on this problem. Now granted I do a half-ass job and maybe save you a little money by not using veneers, but we're talking about your overall health and well-being. Your smile is one of the best I've seen on deckhands. Would you want to ruin that beautiful smile? Your smile reminds me of The Queen Mary's hair. Supple," said Dr. Dunston.

"Me always thought me had supple smile like The Queen Mary's hair. Me hate to ruin it."

"There you go. 'A pinch and a penny is all I can say, but if you flounder about, it's likely you'll stay,' is what I always say. Now open wide so I can get some measurements," said the Doctor as he placed some cotton balls in his ears. "This is going to hurt, and you're going to scream. In case you were wondering why I was putting cotton balls in my ears."

And now I hear screaming from just down the hall," the captain wrote in his journal as he gazed out the window. *It troubles me so that we are currently heading in the wrong direction. I feel like my life is full of misdirection. My closest friends, are people that constantly challenge my authority. No matter how many times I question their decisions, they always seem to wonder if I'm a good leader. I struggle with that doubt considering my father's father's father was a great captain. Every generation of men in my family commanded a boat, whether they liked it or not. All great captains of industry. Like me. Oh journal. I struggle with the fact we haven't seen a whale in nearly six weeks. I feel that the sea is baron of those moronic beasts. Will anything ever go my way? My sickness is getting worse. I tried sleeping south verses north like Dr. Dunston suggested. It was very fleeting. Oh, how I wonder if my sea sickness will ever end? Journal, I think I need rest. I am willing to try anything to get my sea legs. I have tried sleeping north, and I've tried sleeping south. Maybe I will try sleeping east. The direction we are currently travelling. It seems like that's the only way.* Captain Limb set down his ink feather before lying down to rest.

Below deck, Dunky gazed at a handful of blueberries. As he picked one from the bunch, he examined and said to himself, "So round. Round like that cannonball. Something just doesn't add up. When me look at the moon, it's round too. Why can't the earth be round?" said Dunky to himself quietly. "What you talking about? You talking to yourself?" asked a nearby deckhand. "Yeah. I was just thinking. Thinking to myself." "What are you thinking about?" asked the deckhand.

"Me just thinking about how round things are," Dunky said.

"Round like me head? Me head is round, right?" asked the deckhand.

"Exactly. Look at our heads. Our heads are round."

"Dunky, me get what you're saying about round things. Me think it's great you have these wild dreams about the world being round. But me have a real problem. Me lost me harpoon again. In fact, most of my other deckhands lost theirs too. We just don't have any simple way to retrieve them. Most of us can't swim. So when we throw our harpoons in the water, they sink into the sea," said the deckhand. Dunky thought for a second.

"We need a way to somehow throw our harpoons and have them come back automatically," Dunky said as he paused for a second to gather his thoughts.

"One time me met an … who carried a thing called a boomerang. He would throw it at these creatures called Kuala Bears that hopped around on their hind legs me think. Anyway, the only way he could hunt was to throw this boomerang. It would whack the Kuala bear in the brains, then the boomerang would come right back," said Dunky. What if me bent your harpoon, like a boomerang, and you gave this thing a toss. In theory, you and the boys could throw these boomer-poons, whack the whale in the brains and it would come right back to you?"

"Well Almighty Damn. That sounds amazing," said the deckhand.

"Perfect. You go up and grab everyone's harpoons and we'll get these things converted over to boomer-poons as soon as possible."

"Aye, aye, Dunky," said the deckhand as he ran upstairs to tell everyone the good news.

As the sun started to set on The Queen Mary, the Cog, a blue jay flew just above the waterline towards the bow. "New jay coming in," yelled one of the deckhands as the blue jay landed on railing near First Lieutenant. The First Lieutenant grabbed the jay and peeled the jay message off his little leg and threw him back in the air.

"From The Queen Mary - Where are you? I'm waiting," said the jay.

"Oh, this is not good," First Lieutenant said as he looked around the deck. The Queen Mary was clearly upset about their whereabouts and they have been travelling in the wrong direction for days. Our storage hulls literally contain zero percent jam. The Queen Mary is going to skin us alive, First Lieutenant thought as beads of sweat started to form on his brow. "Does anyone know Captain Limb's whereabouts?" he asked one of the deckhands that was happening to walk past. "He's napping, me believe," said the deckhand.

"Well, that's just great. I'll let him sleep, but we need to solve this problem as soon as possible," said First Lieutenant.

As the sun rose over the horizon a new day dawned on The Queen Mary, The Cog's journey. The captain woke with a bad taste in his mouth and a slight upset stomach. Oh, hopefully this is going to be a good day," he thought as he put on his captain's boots and straightened his captain's patch.

"Has anyone seen First Lieutenant this morning? I'm wondering what the news of the day is," he yelled to a passing deckhand.

"Me thinks me saw him on the top deck," said the deckhand as he swept the floor just outside the captain's quarters.

"Great. I'll take a blueberry tea, with a nice muffin if you don't mind," said the captain. The deckhand just stared at him blindly as he walked.

"Well, me only sweep floors, but me guess me'll give someone the message?" The deckhand muttered to himself in confusion.

"Good morning, Captain Limb," First Lieutenant said as he finished tying a sailors knot in a nearby rope. "Good morn to you. What's the news of the day? How is the ship performing?" asked the Captain. "The ship is performing great. There are no holes to report. The sails are nice and white. All the ropes have knots. The anchor is polished and the decks have been swabbed," said First Lieutenant.

"Wonderful. And the crew. How is my crew doing this morning?"

"Spirts are high. Morale is high. Everyone always says that this is their favorite cog to work on," said First Lieutenant.

"The Queen Mary, the Cog is a wonderful ship to command," Captain Limb agreed. "So, any other news?"

"Well. We're still heading eastward. I don't know if you recall, but we received a jay from The Queen Mary several days ago asking us to turn back towards Pottstown to pick up a supply of blueberry jam."

"Did we pick up the jam?" interrupted the Captain. Looking confused First Lieutenant said, "No, we never turned around. You said you were going to come up with a solution. So we never got the jam? We have no jam on board," said the captain.

"Not a single ounce," said First Lieutenant.

"Well. We need to turn around as soon as possible, and get the jam," yelled Captain Limb.

"Great. So you want us to turn around? I like that decision. It's very clear and precise. There is just one thing though," said First Lieutenant.

"What now?" said the captain.

"Well. The thing is. We got another jay yesterday from The Queen Mary asking where are you? It seemed pretty urgent," said First Lieutenant.

"'Where are you,'" the captain repeated. "That seems like she's angry. What is our current mission status," asked the captain?

"Well, we were initially sent on a mission to slaughter and kill blue whales for meat. The Queen Mary then added a side mission of having us visit Pottstown to retrieve a shipment of blueberry jam," said First Lieutenant.

"Those mission seem easy enough. How many have we been successful at?" asked the captain.

"None. We have no whale meat, and our jars are filled with zero percent of jam," said First Lieutenant.

"This is a total disaster. and The Queen Mary wants us to return home immediately," yelled the captain.

"We are going to be in so much trouble if we return to Blueburrie with no whale blubber or blueberry jam. We must come up with a solution and we better hurry and figure out something quick before we make it back," the captain said with a concerned look on his face.

"Blueburrie, ho," yelled a deckhand as he pointed to the horizon.

"Too Late," signed First Lieutenant.

"Shit. I'm going to take a nap," muttered Captain Limb.

Chapter Seven

THE COG'S RETURN

❦

"It's The Queen Mary, the Cog. The Queen Mary, the Cog has returned. Three cheers for The Queen Mary, the Cog," a harbor man shouted as stood on a nearby pier. Since it was pretty early in the morning no one was around to give three cheers, so the harbor man simply cheered himself.

"Hurray, hurray, hurray," he shouted. As the Cog got closer, a deckhand yelled out, "Three masts past the jib line, Harbor man. Lines are tight and knotted,"

"What?" yelled the harbor man.

"Me said, three masts past the jib line," yelled the deckhand.

"Oh. Good," said the harbor man, clearly confused by the deckhands' instructions.

"You want me to park next to that fishing vessel?" yelled the deckhand.

"What?" said the harbor man.

"Where should we park?" yelled the deckhand.

"Oh. Yes. Well, I'm not sure. Why don't you just anchor there and swim ashore? We'll sort out the parking situation later. Do you have a dingy you can use?" yelled the Harbor man.

"Huh?" said the deckhand.

"Dingy. A small boat you typically tow behind your larger boat?" screamed the harbor man.

"Oh. Dingy. Yes. But it's full of cannonball holes. We use it as target practice," yelled the deckhand.

"What?" yelled the harbor man

"Target practice. We use it as target practice," yelled the deckhand.

"Oh," said the harbor man. Confused and slightly annoyed by the whole situation, the harbor man picked up his chum bucket and went about his business.

****

"This cell is cold and scary," said Flounder as he sat next to Ray down in the castle's dungeon.

"I'm scared too," said Ray as he put his hand on Flounder's shoulder. As the two best acquaintances sat next to each other on the dungeon cell floor they could hear the slight sound of rats squeaking, water dripping and the occasional scream from someone being tortured. Flounder was right in his assessment of the dungeon being scary. The Queen Mary took great pleasure in decorating the castle's dungeon and added fake spider webs, spiders made from yarn, and the occasional rubber snake to intimidate anyone that was being punished and held there.

"Is that a snake?" Flounder said as he looked out the cell door into the hallway.

"Let me see. If it is, it's probably sleeping. It hasn't moved since we got here," said Ray.

"I hate snakes. Spiders too. Ray, I'm cold. Do you think I could have the lower half of my shirt back?" asked Flounder as he pointed to his bare midriff.

"I should probably keep it on, Flounder. It's part of my outfit for tap dancing and if The Queen Mary calls me back to try again, I should be ready, don't you think?" said Ray.

"You're probably right. It's just my midriff. I'm sure if I think about warm places, my body will warm up," as Flounder started to shiver.

"Ray. What happened at the ball? I thought your dancing was majestic. I don't understand why The Queen Mary was so upset," Flounder said as he grabbed his legs for warmth.

"I think it was my paradiddle. I knew that I should have practiced that more," Ray said as he started to shed a tear.

"It's okay. I think your paradiddle is great, Ray. You're the best paradiddler I know."

"Thanks, Flounder. You are the best acquaintance I know, "Ray said as he adjusted his hand made cummerbund.

****

"The Queen Mary. The Queen Mary. The Queen Mary, the Cog has returned," Margarine yelled as she ran in to her bedroom.

The Queen Mary, still in her pajamas sprung out bed. "What? The Queen Mary, the Cog? Captain Limb is back." She danced around in circles with her arms high in the air.

"I can see the ship now in the harbor. The deckhands are swimming ashore as we speak," said Margarine as she looked out the castle window.

"Move aside simpleton and let me look," The Queen Mary commanded. "Oh my, what a wonderful site. That ship is so majestic. You know what makes that ship so special?" she asked.

Margarine thought for a second and said, "It's size?"

"Nope, guess again," said The Queen Mary.

"It's crew?"

"Nope. Guess again," said The Queen Mary.

"It's color?"

"Wrong again."

"It's function?"

"Not even close," said the Queen Mary.

Margarine thought for a second and said, "Its ability to catch and kill whales?" she asked.

59

"Still wrong, dumb, dumb," The Queen Mary said as she snickered.

"The fact that The Queen Mary, the Cog, is so ahead of its time? Being that it's only the year 528 AD and historically speaking this type of ship won't be developed for another four hundred years or so?" asked Margarine.

"Wrong. You simpleton. It's the sculpture. The beautiful sculpture of me riding a peacock on the front of the ship known as the aft," said The Queen Mary. Margarine shrugged and simply nodded in agreement.

"Now get me my best blue schmock and call my guards. I must head to see Captain Limb at once."

****

The door at NumNucks busts open and Hu ran inside. "Did you all hear the good news? The Queen Mary, the Cog, has returned. Captain Limb is back. I have no doubt in my mind he's brought us at least two blue whales. Do you know how much meat that will provide the town? Whale tongue, whale tail, whale flippers. My mouth is watering just thinking about all the options,." he screamed as he sat down at the bar.

"Who are you talking about?" asked NumNuck as he cleaned a glass behind the bar.

"Captain Limb. The famous whale killing captain," Hu said as he pointed at an Ale behind the bar.

"Captain Tim?" NumNuck said.

"No. Captain Limb. He's been in this bar a hundred times. Not to mention every time he comes to port his crew of forty deckhands drink here," said Hu.

"Listen. I can't remember everyone's name that comes in the bar. It's just not that type of place," NumNuck said as he poured an ale for Hu.

"Well. I guess it doesn't really matter. I'm just so excited to get something other than Peacock in my butcher shop. I'll bet you, he got six whales. Big ones too. I can't wait." As Hu slugged his beer and threw one penaoloid down on the bar. "Keep the change. I've got some knife sharpening to do. Whale meat, whale meat in my belly. I can't wait for whale meat, Sally," said Hu.

"My name isn't Sally, it's NumNuck."

"I know, I was talking to Sally," He waved to Sally in the back of the bar. "See you later. Stop by the butcher shop early. That whale meat is going to fly off the shelves," said Hu.

As Mosh headed down fourth avenue he glanced at all the garbage that was left behind by the ball the previous night. "They left out the potato salad. Figures. That'll never keep," Mosh says to himself as he reached down to pick up some decorations. "What a bunch of animals. I can't believe they left the square like this. What type of animal spills their ale and doesn't clean it up?" Mosh says. He looks over at a group of peafowl eating some of the left-over blueberry crumb cake. "Did anyone think to wrap up the crumb cake so the Almighty damned peacocks wouldn't eat it?" he yelled to no one in particular. "This is probably going to take me all morning to clean up," said Mosh.

"Hey Mosh. Did you hear the good news?" said Mrs. Warwick as she crossed the street.

"What good news? Look at this mess. What a bunch of pigs. I swear people are trying to kill me," said Mosh.

"Oh my, you didn't hear the good news. Captain Limb is back. I can only assume he's brought delicious blue whale meat. He's probably dragging those beautiful dead angry beasts on to the shore now," said Mrs. Warwick.

"Did anyone think to put down some tarps before he does that? He's going to stain all the beaches with whale blood if he doesn't," yelled Mosh. "I swear to the Almighty, if they think I'm going to clean up this mess, and have to clean blood off the beach, they're nuts. I'm not doing it. I won't do it. I can't do it. Holy Moses. When do I have time for any of this?" screamed Mosh.

"Well. I'm just excited about the whale tongue. It's my favorite," said Mrs. Warwick.

Near the north end of Blueburrie, Toss was busy packing to head back to the Dominades. He had received a jay earlier in the morning that he was urgently needed to be on the next sailing vessel as soon as possible. Toss grabbed his alligator boots and threw his favorite converting knife into his satchel. "That should do it," he said flipping the bag over and tightening the straps. "Time to get back to Operation Convert. Accept or die," a campaign that The Queen Mary had initiated a few years earlier. Toss closed the door to The Vacation Inn and headed down fourth avenue towards the harbor.

"Well Almighty Damned," Toss said to himself as he got closer to the Harbor. That looks like The Queen Mary, The Cog. I've never seen her up close before. What a majestic ship, he thought.

"Me like your boots," a deckhand said as he walked pass Toss.

"Thanks. I took them off a dead non-believer. You wouldn't happen to know if there's a ship heading for the Dominades by any chance?" Toss asked.

"Me pretty sure that Carrack is leaving now. You better hurry," said the Deckhand.

"Thanks. Alligator boots don't fail me now," as Toss ran towards the ship just about to leave. Running down the pier as fast as he can he noticed the Carrack just starting to pull away from the dock.

"Wait for me. Wait for me," he cried as he threw his satchel to a deckhand aboard the Carrack.

"Jump for it, My Friend. Jump." Toss ran as long as he could before leaping from the dock. He barely caught the hands of a couple deckhands.

"You're one lucky son of a peahen," one of the deckhands said.

"No kidding. I can't wait to get back to converting,'" said Toss.

Near the entrance of the castle a column of guards assembled. In the middle of the column was a horse buggy cart strapped to three guards. The Queen Mary was notorious for disliking the way horses smell so she insisted the guards pull her cart instead.

"The Queen Mary approaches," said one of the guards.

The Queen Mary walked majestically to the cart and climbed in. "Guards, head to the harbor at once. I must greet Captain Limb personally and congratulate him on his victory over the vicious blue whale," said The Queen Mary. "Make it be known that we are travelling through the streets."

The column of guards proceeded out the castle keep door. "Move. Scatter. Disperse. Move. Scatter. Disperse," some chanted as they moved briskly down fourth ave. A few guards screeched like peacocks to deter any from crossing the road. If one accidently did the guards would kick them as hard as they could to discourage any other peacocks. "Move. Scatter. Disperse," they yelled as the column got closer to the harbor. The Queen Mary sat dignified as the guards pulled her cart through the street.

"Look once, look twice, no guards in sight, proceed," Mrs. Warrick said to herself as she took a step on to fourth avenue. As she slowly walked across the street, The Queen Mary's guarded procession appeared around the corner. "Move. Scatter. Disperse," the guards screamed at her.

"I'm moving. I'm trying to scatter. I'm in the process of dispersing," Mrs. Warwick yelled.

"Move. Scatter. Disperse," they yelled as they got within pushing distance.

"I'm trying," said Mrs. Warwick. She did her best to scamper across the street. Unfortunately, it was too late. Two guards broke off the column, grabbed Mrs. Warwick, and threw her aside. The rest of the column proceeded down the street. The Queen Mary yelled, "Stop," bringing the column of guards to a halt.

"Why didn't you disperse?" The Queen Mary asked Mrs. Warick.

"I tried. I was trying my best to disperse. I couldn't do it fast enough," she cried.

"Enough. How many times have I told the people of Blueburrie to practice, practice, practice their dispersing?" The Queen Mary asked while looking down at Mrs. Warwick.

Mrs. Warwick started to sigh. "You tell us about every Wednesday during your town lectures," she said.

"And," The Queen Mary scolded.

"And Saturdays and Sundays during your hall meetings, you remind us to practice our dispersing," said Mrs. Warwick.

"Exactly. I constantly remind you how important it is to disperse when my column of guards approaches. It's for your safety. Not mine. If I'm in a hurry and you get run over, it won't be my fault. It's your fault. For The Queen Mary is divine and should never have to stop for anyone or anything," she said .

"I am very sorry. I'll never let it happen again," said Mrs. Warwick.

"I'm sure you won't since you'll have plenty of time to practice your dispersing in the Castle Dungeon. Guards. You know what to do. Take. Her. Away."

"No. Don't take me away. Who's going to feed my chartreux?" screamed Mrs. Warwick.

"No one will," The Queen Mary laughed. "Your chartreux will probably starve because you didn't disperse. Again, not my problem," The Queen Mary snickered. "Guards proceed to the harbor," she yelled.

****

"Does anyone know if the captain has awoken from his nap yet?" said First Lieutenant.

"Me not sure," said one of the deckhands and he tip toed quietly past First Lieutenant.

"Does anyone know why we haven't parked the Cog yet? Why are we sitting in the middle of the harbor?" First Lieutenant said as he walked past a bunch of deckhands sitting quietly on the deck.

"We don't have a parking spot yet. We're still waiting for a pier to open up. We were told to stay seated and stay quiet until we've come to a complete stop," said another deckhand.

"I see. Well, I suppose there's nothing we can do but wait."

"Wait for what?" said the captain as he rubbed the sleep from his eyes.

"Oh, Sir. Nice to see you. We're waiting for a parking spot to open up," said First Lieutenant.

"Well. Nothing we can do about that. We'll just have to stay seated and wait patiently," said Captain Limb.

"Exactly what I was just saying to the deckhands," said First Lieutenant.

"I'm sure you were. It's pretty much standard procedure. Surprises me actually that you would even have to remind them," said Captain Limb as he took a sip of his blueberry tea.

"What's the news? How's the ship? How's the crew?" asked the captain.

"I'm glad you asked. The ship is currently parked in the harbor. As I said earlier, we're waiting for a parking spot. The crew is in high spirits and is remaining seated," said First Lieutenant.

"Very well. How high are their spirits?" asked Captain Limb.

"Very high. Very high indeed. They are very excited to be home and visit with family and even stop by NumNucks and have a fresh ale," said First Lieutenant.

"Yes, NumNucks. I'm afraid I get a little bashful going in there. NumNuck always makes such a big deal out of my presence. I embarrass easily," said Captain Limb.

"So, what's the news?" "Well, we still have those two slight problems," said First Lieutenant.

"Problems?" asked the captain.

"Yes. Well, the fact that we have no blueberry jam on board and not a single ounce of whale meat. I'm sure The Queen Mary is going to be less than amused at our lack of performance in the whale and jam departments," said First Lieutenant. Captain Limb took one sip of his tea and looked around the deck.

"Is there any way we can fudge our jam? Does anyone have any jam?" as he looked at a bunch of deckhands sitting near the bow of the Cog. "Toe?" asked one of the deckhands.

"No, not to jam, Blueberry," yelled the captain.

"No," they replied.

"Does anyone have any whale meat? Preferably blue," yelled the captain. The deckhands simply shrugged.

"This puts us really in a jam. Does The Queen Mary know we're here?" ask Captain Limb.

"I believe she's well aware. In fact I can see her column of guards coming down Fourth Avenue now," said First Lieutenant.

"Holy almighty, shit," yelled the captain. "I'm going down to take a nap. If The Queen Mary comes let her know I'm sleeping. This should buy us some time."

Chapter Eight

THE DUNGEON

The door opened to Dungeon level three, and two guards led Mrs. Warwick to her cell. "I'd like a cell with a view of the castle garden, if possible," said Mrs. Warwick as they led her down the dungeon hallway.

"We only have views of the larder," said one of the Guards.

"I suppose that'll do. Will I have to share a cell with anyone?" asked Mrs. Warwick.

"We have a slight overcrowding issue currently at the dungeon. I'm afraid you will have to share," said the Guard.

"Well, this day couldn't get any worse," Mrs. Warwick says as she adjusts her shackles. The occasional groan and moan filled the silence of the dungeon hall.

"We're here. Open cell X. V. I. I. I." yelled the guard.

"What cell?" asked another guard.

"X.V.I.I.I" repeated the guard.

"X.V.I.V?"

"No! X. V. I. I. I" yelled the guard.

"What? X. What?"

"Just open cell 18!" screamed the guard in frustration as he removed Mrs. Warwick's shackles. The door opened to Ray and Flounder huddled in the cell.

"Ray. Flounder. Am I glad to see you. I thought I'd have to bunk with a stranger," said Mrs. Warwick.

"Mrs. Warwick. What in the world are you doing here?". asked Ray.

"I didn't disperse. They got me on a non-dispersing charge," Mrs. Warwick said as the guards closed the door behind her.

"Not again. Well welcome to cell 18. We're happy you're here," said Flounder.

"Thanks. I guess," said Mrs. Warwick

"Ray, when do you think The Queen Mary will let us out? I have a dentist appointment on Thursday," asked Flounder.

"I'm not entirely sure," said Ray. "I really messed up bad. I knew I should have practiced more. I'm not even sure if I'll ever get to tap again," Ray said as he started to cry.

"Don't say that," Mrs. Warwick said. "You've been tapping since you were a baby. I remember changing your diapers and you would always tap your feet on the table while I wiped your behind," Mrs. Warwick said.

"Yeah, Ray, I agree. I wasn't there to change your diapers, but there's been plenty of times you've drank too much, and I've helped you clean your shorts when you've soiled yourself. I wouldn't know what to do if I didn't hear your tappers tap," said Flounder.

"Flounder, you and Mrs. Warwick are right. I know my taps. And I have confidence in my shoes. Hopefully The Queen Mary will respect that and let us go soon," said Ray.

"I think she will," said Flounder.

Down the hall in cell 84 a small man by the name of Porksmu rolled some lint he had collected into a small ball. Spotting a spider web in the corner, Porksmu stood up and collected the web to create a string to attach to the lint ball. Now the size of a golf ball, it would be a perfect toy for his pet cat Mr. Wriggly, who would often visit him sneaking through the cell window at night. Porksmu had been serving a multi-year sentence for failure to bow when ordered to by The Queen Mary. His defense was always that since The Queen Mary has a lazy eye, he wasn't sure that she was looking directly at him when she made the order. To this day, he always would respond with a "Who me?" type of statement whenever anyone would confront him about anything. Despite that, Porksmu was quite the inventor. He could make just about anything out of nothing. His cell certainly showed that. Having lived alone for several years, he had the luxury of being able to build and invent. Using his creativity, he was able to deconstruct his bed in to a beautiful four-piece dining room set complete with table and four chairs. He removed the whale oil from his night lamp to grease the hinges of his cell door so it wouldn't squeak. He even constructed a yoga mat from random peacock feathers that would fly in his window late at night. Everyone in the dungeon knew, if you wanted to get something made, Porksmu was your man.

"Feeding time. Feeding time," yelled one of the guards. He moved over to the master lever and pulled as hard as he could which opened all the cell doors. "Proceed straightly and orderly and fashionably towards the feed hall," the guard commanded. Ray, Flounder, and Mrs. Warwick rose to their feet and exited their cell. Everyone lined up and proceeded through the musty hallways down a flight of steps towards a large hall. Above the door to the hall was a sign that read "Kids Eat Free." As Ray, Flounder, and Mrs. Warwick moved toward the front of the feed line they grabbed their plates, spoon, fork, and soup spoon.

"Don't forget your salad fork," the guard said as the three proceeded through the line.

"I can tell you're all new at this," said the guard.

"Oh Almighty. Lobster again. I'm so sick of shellfish. Can't they feed us some fowl?" Porksmu whispered to Ray who was standing in front of him.

"Make sure you grab a small cup of that melted butter to dunk it in. It makes that rubbery meat go down easier," said Porksmu.

"You want any bisque?" the Guard asked Flounder as he stepped next in line.

"Bisque? What's bisque?" asked Flounder.

"It's seafood, or we have clam chowder," said the guard.

"Can I have neither? I'm seafood intolerant," said Flounder.

"Nope, you must pick one. The Queen Mary insists her prisoners are fed."

"I'll take the chowder," said Flounder.

Ray, Flounder, and Mrs. Warwick turned and found an empty table. They sat down nervously and began to eat. "This food is disgusting," said Ray.

"I agree. The lobster is so chewy, it's hard for me to swallow. What I wouldn't give for a nice cold peacock sandwich," said Mrs. Warwick.

"You've had a peacock sandwich lately?" Porksmu interrupted as he sat down at the table. "I haven't had peacock for years. Every once in a while, a peacock feather will fly into my cell and I try and suck them to get a taste of the flavor, but it's not the same," Porksmu said.

"I just had peacock yesterday. Extra juicy," said Mrs. Warwick.

"That sounds divine like," said Porksmu. "I should really introduce myself. My name is Porksmu. I'm pretty much the go to guy around here if you need or want anything. You name it and I can make it."

"You think you could make me a cummerbund? Just like Rays?" Flounder interrupted.

"No problem," said Porksmu.

"That would be great. My midriff is freezing in this damp dungeon," said Flounder.

"Do you think you could make me one too?" asked Ray. "I wonder if it was this specific cummerbund that threw off my tapping and that's the reason why The Queen Mary didn't like my routine? If I have a new cummerbund maybe I can tap better," said Ray.

"I probably only have the materials to make one," said Porksmu.

"Go ahead, Porksmu. Make Ray's first," said Flounder. "I don't need one, like he does. I'll be okay," said Flounder while still shivering.

"Feeding complete," yelled one of the guards. "Please stand, bow to one another, and let's proceed to the exercise yard. Knees up."

Ray, Flounder, Mrs. Warwick, and Porksmu stood to form a line. The line of prisoners began to walk raising their knees with each step. They left the feed hall and proceeded single file to the exercise yard where the prisoners were free to walk about and associate with one another. Upon arriving at the exercise yard, the four decided to sit at a picnicking table that was outside underneath a blueberry tree.

"That sun feels nice," said Flounder.

"It sure is a nice day," said Mrs. Warwick.

"Mrs. Warwick, Is that you?" said Hu. He walked up to the picnic table.

"Why yes, yes I am Mrs. Warwick," she said realizing she was talking to Hu.

"Hu, what are you doing here? Are you just visiting and possibly catering dinner later on?" she asked.

"I wish," said Hu. "Unfortunately, I have been detained for mushy peacock bones. During the ball The Queen Mary found a mushy bone in her pulled-peacock sandwich. I wasn't there, but as you know, the law states that any mushy peacock bones found in any peacock dinner, that I am to be responsible. It's a law I've been trying to change for years. Alas, it was too late," said Hu.

"Oh, that is so unfortunate. You're too young to rot your life away in this dungeon," said Mrs. Warwick.

"I'm hoping that during Judgement Hour the Queen Mary will forgive me for my actions," said Hu.

"Let's hope so. She can be very decisive," said Mrs. Warwick.

"Steaming time. Please visit the changing rooms and put on your steam attire," yelled the guards.

"Now we have to go for a steam?" said Mrs. Warwick. "What's next? Massages?" she said jokingly.

"After your daily steam, remember to keep your attire on for your massage," yelled the guard.

"Ray, I'm bashful about my nipples. If we have to get daily massages, I'm nervous," said Flounder.

"I know, Flounder. Does anyone know if the massages are full frontal?" asked Ray.

"They certainly are," said one of the guards.

Flounder nervously looked at Ray as the two walked towards the steam room. "This place is a nightmare," said Flounder.

"I agree. I'm just as scared," said Ray.

Mrs. Warwick, Flounder, and Ray began walking single file down the dungeon hallway where, what Ray and Flounder assumed was smoke, appeared to be coming from the door near the end. Neither of them had ever seen steam before.

"Is the place on fire?" asked Ray. "Where are they sending us? I feel hot. I'm starting to get sweaty. My cummerbund is getting moist," yelled Ray.

"They're going to steam us alive," yelled Flounder.

"I think it feels quite nice. If this is the way I die, I'm fine with it," said Mrs. Warwick. The three follow the line and enter the steam room. Along the wall are tiered level benches full of prisoners. It was hard to see through the thick fog of steam, but hesitantly Mrs. Warwick, Ray, and Flounder found a seat.

"Oh, excuse me," said Flounder as he sat on Pom's lap. "No problem, it's quite hard to see in here because of all the steam," said Pom.

"Pom, Is that you?" said Flounder.

"Flounder, is that you?"

"Yeah, it's me, Flounder."

"It's me, Pom?"

"What on the flat earth are you doing here?" said Flounder. At that moment noticing Gil sitting next to Pom.

"We were detained. Apparently, The Queen Mary was snacking on a bag of our sun-dried blueberries. She had strong feelings that they were merely sun-kissed and not sun-dried," said Gil.

"I mentioned I thought that they weren't up to her standards," said Pom.

"That you did. At any rate, sun-kissed blueberries are a punishable crime in Blueburrie so we were arrested late last night."

"I barely had time to put on my slacks," said Gil.

"The Queen Mary's guards were pretty aggressive, but we deserved it," said Pom.

"They weren't just pretty aggressive, they were very aggressive," said Gil

"Massage time. Form a line, single file, and proceed downstairs to the parlor," yelled one of the guards.

"I don't know if I can take much more of this. Seafood for lunch. Exercise. Steams. Massages. I can't wait until Judgement Hour. They're torturing us," said Flounder.

"I just want things to get back to normal. I just want to be able to watch you practice your tap dancing and eat peacock and blueberries. Like we used. Yesterday," whispered Flounder to Ray in front of him.

"It has been a very long day," said Ray. "Hopefully when The Queen Mary has judgement hour, she'll go easy on our sentence."

Leading the way, Ray walked into the massage parlor where several prisoners were already getting massages. Prisoners groaned and moaned in pain. "My vertebral," one screamed out.

"Pick a table and lay down," said one of the guards.

"If you're wearing shoes, remove them so we don't get any peacock sit on the slabs," said another guard. Mrs. Warwick took the furthest slab from the door while Ray and Flounder grabbed two slabs that were next to each other. Laying down, face first, they braced for their message.

"Hold my hand," said Ray as he looked to Flounder.

"I won't let go. I'll never let go," cried Flounder. The two braced as two skinny female guards squirted warm oil on their backs and began to rub.

"It hurts," yelled Ray.

"Me too," yelled Flounder as the two began to cry.

Chapter Nine

THE QUEEN MARY VERSES THE QUEEN MARY, THE COG

C rouched down behind a barrel First Lieutenant whispers to a deckhand passing by, "Has The Queen Mary arrived yet?"

"Me don't think so," the deckhand said, crouching next to him. "Why are we crouching?" asked the deckhand.

"I'm scared of The Queen Mary," said First Lieutenant. "When she finds out we failed in our mission she's going to send us all to the dungeon,"

"Me hears that they force you to eat lobster and the bunks don't even have any foam toppers," said the deckhand.

"I heard the same. I'll tell you one thing. The captain certainly isn't going to nap through this one. He had every opportunity to turn the ship around when The Queen Mary requested it. I really feel like I should say something if questioned," said First Lieutenant.

"You totally should. This one time, me was minding my own business when Flug, do you know Flug?" asked the deckhand.

"Flug? I'm not sure. Is he a deckhand?" said First Lieutenant.

"Yeah, he's a deckhand on the quarter deck."

"I'm not sure. You all look very similar to me," said First Lieutenant.

"Well, anyway, Flug, walked pass I and accused I of eating his pulled peacock sandwich. Me saw it in the cooler box and me knew it was his. Me never touched the thing. Well, anyway, Flug starts swinging his arms, and kicking his feet and legs. Me thought he was having a seizure, so me let him be. But it turns out. He wanted to fight I. Me started to spin in circles, trying to confuse him. Me suspect it worked because he stopped his crazy motions. He warned I If me ever ate his sandwich again, he'd punch I, kill I, and toss me corpse over the side of the Cog," said the deckhand.

"What did you say? I'm sorry. I wasn't listening," said First Lieutenant.

"Me forgot," said the deckhand.

"No matter. Let me know as soon as The Queen Mary arrives," said First Lieutenant.

"Yes sir," said the deckhand.

"Move. Scatter. Disperse," the guards yelled as the column walked down Fourth avenue towards the harbor. Sitting in the cart was The Queen Mary, looking through some portraits drawn by Floru the night before at the ball. This certainly was a lovely ball, thought The Queen Mary. One of the better ones. Very few arrests, she thought. Roasted peacock, alive peacock, peahen, some of my friends dancing. Oh, here's a very nice portrait of Toss inspiring some children to join the Dominades. He's such a good influence. I should send him a jay with some words of encouragement, she thought. "Move. Scatter. Disperse," one of the guards yelled as he kicked a peahen out of the way.

"I enjoy this portrait of my new friends Gimlett and Morehouse. Here's another portrait of a pile of blueberries on the floor. I'm surprised no one decided to eat those. They look very sweet and divine," The Queen Mary said to herself. "What a wonderful portrait of Blur. My how he is enjoying himself lying face down on the dancefloor. He must have slipped on some peacock pebbles. I like that portrait," The Queen Mary's column of guards continued to march down Fourth Avenue.

"Halt," screamed The Queen Mary as they approached Blur sitting on the side of Fourth Avenue rubbing his temples. "Blur.

How are you today? How is everything going at the butcher shop," The Queen Mary asked.

"I haven't been yet. I woke up just now. I'm a little confused and dazed to be quite honest," said Blur.

"The roasted peacock was divine last night. My only complaint is that I did get one mushy bone, and I'm sure you heard that we arrested your nephew last night in accordance with the law," said The Queen Mary.

"You what? Arrested? The law? Mushy?"

"Yes. Mushy bone. The mushy bone I found in my pulled peacock sandwich. I sent a team of sixteen guards over to your butcher shop late last night. I instructed them to smash your windows and rub the remaining supplies of blueberry jam all over your shop. Thank the Almighty that Captain Limb has returned just in time with a fresh supply," said The Queen Mary.

"Did my nephew resist?" asked Blur.

"Not in the slightest. But I wanted my guards to make a point and set an example. You are never to serve me mushy bones again. For I am The Queen Mary. Divine."

"I understand," interrupted Blur while rubbing the sleep from his eyes. "Did the guards at least lock the door to the butcher shop before they left?" asked Blur

"Nope. Carry on. Onward to the Harbor," said The Queen Mary.

****

Dearest Journal, Captain Limb began writing. *We arrived back in the harbor of Blueburrie today. We are currently in the process of waiting for a parking spot to open up, and have moored the cog dead center in the harbor for all to see. The ship is nearly as majestic as The Queen Mary herself. I am so proud of myself, the crew and how the ship has performed over the last several months. We sailed directly west for several months and then decided to turn around 180 degrees back to the east. The ship turned spot on, and never hesitated. The crew is one of the best crews I've had in a long time. Despite their inability to properly use first person pronouns I find it rather charming when a deckhand will say something like 'Me finger is in his ear.' or 'Me thinks we're going to hit that coral, Captain.' They do work hard and they are very obedient. I often will bark out a ridiculous order just to see if they will abide. Nearly 1 hundred percent of the time, they fall directly in line and do what they're told,* the captain wrote.

First Lieutenant has been both my right—and left—hand man throughout this journey. He is very thorough and provides information to me using words that he generates using his mouth. Most of the time I understand what he's saying, but there are times where I have no idea what he is trying to convey. During these times of conversation I hesitate to ask questions. I find we make a great team because he uses his words to describe situations to me and I answer back using words as well. While the crew has been an absolute blessing to be with, this has been one of the hardest journeys of my life. My sea sickness never quite subsided and I'm looking forward to getting my feet on some solid flat earth ground. It seems every time I step aboard a sailing vessel my stomach tightens and my acid reflux refluxes. Most days are surrounded by chronic diarrhea and no matter how much salty water I drink, I never seem to quench my thirst. The sickness that plagues me when I sail does not deter me from staying the course and continuing on, no matter how many bad decisions I make. Sailing is in my gut. I am the proud grandson of a great captain. The captains Limb before me give me strength even when I have uncontrollable diarrhea," The captain gave one more dab of ink to his peacock feather. *For that. I am truly grateful."*

****

"Next," Dr Dunston said as he wiped the blood from his examination table.

"Oh, if it isn't my favorite deckhand. Let me see that beautiful smile of yours. Are you still in considerable pain?" asked Dr. Bluefish.

"Me, pain isn't too bad. It's me sea legs. Since we've arrived back in port, me'd like to get me land legs," said the Deckhand.

"I'm glad you stopped in early about this. It's going to get pretty busy down here with everyone wanting to get their land legs once they get off the cog," said Dr. Dunston.

"Have you thought about the non-surgery option?"

"You mean you won't have to detach me legs?" asked the Deckhand.

"Exactly. We have a new non-intrusive method that actually relies on medication, verses amputation. By placing this sticky patch on your legs it releases endorphins into your bloodstream that will convert your sea legs into land legs. It's my patented formula and it's fairly priced. If it were up to me, medication is the way to go," said Dr. Dunston

"As long as me legs work, me guess that's me best option," said the Deckhand. "Oh, trust me. They won't just work, with those endorphinized legs you'll be skipping and jumping and hopping and running all over town," laughed Dr Dunston.

"Dancing too?" asked the Deckhand.

"Oh. No. Definitely not dancing. But you'll probably get a decent amount of prancing in. Either way, I think it's the way to go. I'll have the captain deduct the cost of the patches from your pay."

****

"Cast the lines and forward the aft about," yelled one of the deckhands.

"Huzzah! We finally have a parking space," yelled another deckhand.

"Is it okay to stand and no longer be silent?" asked another. "Aye, aye," yelled another deckhand.

"Ease her in boys. Ease her in. Don't let your jigs get the best of ya," said First Lieutenant.

The Queen Mary, the Cog began to inch forward towards the dock. Sailing pass the navigational buoys, the mighty cog, squeezed gently in between two other ships anchored at dock.

"Are we approaching straightly?" asked First Lieutenant.

"Define, straightly," yelled a nearby deckhand.

"Not crooked," yelled First Lieutenant.

"Mostly," yelled another deckhand.

"Mostly crooked or mostly straightly?" asked First Lieutenant.

"Mostly both," yelled another deckhand.

The Cog continued forward now getting closer and closer to the dock.

"Bump her off the dock and we'll tie her down tightly. Make sure you use bowline knots instead of halter hitches," yelled First Lieutenant.

"Smile, stand still, and say butter," yelled Floru to a group of deckhands.

"What for?" asked one of the deckhands.

"It's a portrait card for The Queen Mary," said Floru.

"The Queen Mary? Me's going to be famous," yelled a deckhand.

Word spread quickly that Floru was drawing a new portrait. Many of the deckhands stopped what they were doing and ran to the side of the now parked Queen Mary, the Cog, to pose.

"Get me best side," yelled a deckhand.

"Can me blink?" asked another.

"Try to remain perfectly still and don't blink," said Floru as she continued to draw.

Word had also spread quickly throughout the town that Captain Limb had returned. A significant crowd gathered on the docks where The Queen Mary, the Cog, had parked. "Captain Limb. Captain Limb. Captain Limb," the people chanted. "Whale Meat. Whale Meat. Whale Meat," some other's yelled. "Tastes Good. Really Filling," yelled a bunch of harbor men.

Clearly the people are excited about our arrival. I can only imagine that if we had actually done something for the past six months besides going in a straight line back and forth, they might be even more excited, thought First Lieutenant. I wonder if they'll be disappointed when they find out we don't have a single ounce of whale blubber on board?

****

"Move. Scatter. Disperse," the guards yelled as they entered the harbor. "Move. Scatter. Disperse," they yelled again as they pushed a harbor man aside. "The Queen Mary has arrived. All hail. All hail and bow. If you're unable to bow or need assistance bowing, please raise your hand," the guards yelled. The Queen Mary stepped off of her cart and walked to the head harbor man.

"Tell me harbor man. The Queen Mary, The Cog. Has it arrived?"

"Why yes, your highness. She arrived earlier today. She's on dock XXIII," said the harbor man.

"Who?"

"The Queen Mary," said the harbor man.

"No, I didn't. I'm standing right here. I'm not on dock XXIII?" she said with a puzzled look on her face.

"Oh. I meant, the Cog. The Cog is docked at XXIII," he said.

"Great. Then please bow and let us proceed to the dock to see what treasures Captain Limb has brought us from his adventure."

"The Queen Mary is approaching," said one of the deckhands.

"Shit sauce," said First Lieutenant. "This isn't good. Has anyone seen the captain?"

"He's napping," a deckhand responded.

The Queen Mary's column approached and stopped near the edge of the pier. "Announcing, The Queen Mary requests an audience with Captain Limb of The Queen Mary's navy, The Queen Mary, The Cog," yelled one of the guards.

First Lieutenant, hiding behind the center console on the ship, whispered, "Hide" to some nearby deckhands.

"Where?" asked the deckhands.

"Anywhere," said First Lieutenant.

The deckhands scattered about and ran in all directions looking for a spot to hide.

"Captain Limb. Present yourself. I am The Queen Mary, and I have arrived," the Queen Mary said boastfully. The Cog fell totally silent as the deckhands all hid. The only sound was the occasional flap of a giant sail. Did he not hear me? thought The Queen Mary. She repeated herself with more of emphasis.

"Captain Limb, present yourself. For I am the Queen Mary," she yelled. First Lieutenant peeked over the center console.

"Do you think she's going to leave?" asked one of the deckhands.

"Shh," First Lieutenant scolded.

"Something isn't right. Guard, bring me a blue jay. I must send Captain Limb a jay at once and find out where he is," said The Queen Mary.

A guard walked over and plucked a blue jay roosting in a nearby blueberry bush. The Queen Mary wrote on a small piece of paper, *I'm here* and attached the note to the blue jay's leg. She squeezed the blue jay and tossed him high in the air. The blue jay flew nearly three hundred feet into the air and turned to dive bomb The Queen Mary, the Cog. At the last second, it changed direction and flew directly into the window of Captain Limbs quarters. As he rolled over, Captain Limb found the blue jay perched at the foot of his bed.

"First Lieutenant, First Lieutenant," the captain called out. Hearing his name, First Lieutenant carefully slithered along the deck down the steps to Captain Limb's quarters, making sure he wasn't spotted.

"Yes, Captain," he whispered.

"Oh, what a wonderful nap I had. How many hours was I out?" "Several," First Lieutenant whispered.

"Why are you whispering?" asked the captain.

"I'm whispering, because The Queen Mary herself is outside, on the dock."

"What?" Captain Limb shouted.

"The Queen Mary, she's outside," he whispered. "Well, maybe she wants us to leave? What does that jay say?"

"It says, I'm here," said First Lieutenant.

"Do you think she wants to see us?" asked Captain Limb as he rubbed the sleep from his eyes.

"Probably. She keeps yelling your name," said First Lieutenant.

"My name?" asked Captain Limb.

"Yeah. Listen for a second, she keeps screaming your name." The two sat silently for five seconds.

"Captain Limb,"

"See. I think she's calling for you," said First Lieutenant.

"Grab my robe. I better put something on," said Captain Limb.

"I always admired you for napping naked," said First. Lieutenant as he handed him his robe.

"Captain Limb," The Queen Mary screamed now almost losing her voice. Captain Limb presented himself in his velvet robe made of peacock fur.

"I'm here, I'm presenting myself," he said.

"Captain Limb. You have returned. I am so ecstatic to see you. Tell us, tell us about all the tales you've encountered. Both whale and tall. I demand you tell us now. Right now. I am very excited. For I am The Queen Mary. Divine and Excited," she said.

"Well. I have great news. We have sailed for a total of six months. I am happy to report, the seas are filled with salty water. Enough salty water for grandchildren's children's grandchildren to drink. We shall never go thirsty," Captain Limb said.

"Excellent. I love the taste of salty water," said The Queen Mary.

"Our course set us straight west, we sailed nearly three months, until we decided to turn around in fear of falling off the planet earth. So I can confirm that the earth is flat because of our decision," said Captain Limb.

"Very good. Wonderful. I love looking at the earth and how flat it is," said The Queen Mary.

"And, we think we know where the edge of it is, so there's very little chance anyone from the town of Blueburrie will fall off the side," said the captain.

"Yes. Very good point. Very good point indeed," said The Queen Mary.

"After we decided to turn around, we continued in a straight line for three months and we have arrived at home. Safe and sound. In Blueburrie. Mold free," proclaimed Captain Limb as he raised his arms in victory.

"And?" asked The Queen Mary.

"And, and we're looking forward to an epic ball welcoming us home," said the captain, now getting even more nervous.

"A ball filled with whale?" asked The Queen Mary.

"Sure. Whale sounds nice. Does Blur's butcher shop have any frozen whale meat available?" asked the Captain.

"Frozen? Why would I eat frozen when you can offer me fresh?" asked The Queen Mary.

"Well. Here's the thing. The fresh whale meat. You see. We sailed several months in search of the mighty blue whale. But your highness. There simply isn't any left. They either have migrated, or are napping, or have some sort of prejudice against me. Some say they have all swam too far and have fallen off the side of the earth into space. We never saw a single whale. Not blue, not red, not yellow. Nothing. Not a single whale," Captain Limb declared.

"What? Are you trying to make an ass out of me?" yelled The Queen Mary.

"No, I would never do that. I am being as truthful as I can be. My intentions were great. It's my sea sickness. I was ill. I didn't get enough rest. The deckhands made too much noise. First Lieutenant didn't give any updates."

"ENOUGH," yelled The Queen Mary. "I grow tired of your excuses. I should have known when I didn't see any dead whale carcasses on the beach that you failed in your mission. That's the last time I give you the benefit of the doubt. I'm so upset. I am The Queen Mary. I am divine. Majestic."

"That you are," interrupted Captain Limb. "You are all of that and more. I haven't seen you for months and you're even more divine than before."

"Silence," yelled The Queen Mary. "At this point Captain Limb, you have disappointed me. I am not fond of disappointment. I feel like you've let each of my friends down. The whole town of Blueburrie will suffer for your lack of abilities. I'm so upset. Just do me a favor? Load the shipment of blueberry jam you retrieved for me on my royal wagon. The only thing that will cheer me up at this point is a nice fresh slice of toast covered in blueberry jam," said The Queen Mary.

"Well. Here's the thing," said Captain Limb.

First Lieutenant peeked around the console from his hiding spot to see several dozen guards surrounding The Queen Mary. Each guard carried a sword, a side dagger, a whip, and two maces with assorted chains. My Almighty. Those guards are going to kill us. I've got to try and get out of here, he thought. If I have a distraction of some sort, maybe the guards would divert their attention and that would give me just enough time to try and escape and hide. First Lieutenant looked around the Cog, looking for some way to execute what he was calling "Operation Save First Lieutenant." What would be a great distraction? I need something that is a real morale booster that would really impress the guards and The Queen Mary, he thought. Just as First Lieutenant sat and pondered his solution to Operation Save First Lieutenant, Chef Will walked by carrying a satchel full of fresh crawfish.

"That's it," yelled First Lieutenant. I'll organize a cannon target practice at Will, he thought. Everyone gets such joy out of that exercise. That's just the distraction I need. While everyone is focused on our cannonballs whizzing past Chef Will's head, I'll sneak off the boat and hide in that nearby buttery," First Lieutenant said to himself.

"Chef Will. What are you doing?" asked First Lieutenant

"What does it look like? I'm getting the crawfish ready for the gumbo tonight. Why?" said Chef Will.

"I need a favor. I need you to be a huge part in Operation Save First Lieutenant."

"I'm listening," said Chef Will.

"I need you to stop what you're doing."

"But the gumbo," interrupted Chef Will.

"Forget the gumbo. Do you hear The Queen Mary screaming at the captain right now? She's pissed. She was expecting at minimum of twelve blue whales and guess how many we have?" asked First Lieutenant.

"Six?" guessed Chef Will.

"Six? Where do you see six blue whales? No. We have none. This Cog contains zero percent whale meat at the moment. I need a distraction. I'm going to have the deckhands start their cannon target practice. "

"Wait a minute. You want me to go out and be target practice? Again?" Chef Will interrupted as he crouched down besides First Lieutenant still hiding from The Queen Mary.

"It's only one last time. I need a distraction. Listen. I've read your suggestions from the suggestion box. I know how much you hate being target practice. I'm offering you a way out. You and I both know this whole crew is going to suffer when The Queen Mary judges us during judgement hour. There is no way we're getting out of this. We have no whales and no blueberry jam. It's our only way out," said First Lieutenant.

Chef Will thought for a moment. "I guess I have nothing to lose. The deckhands constantly ridicule my food. I've always thought of opening my own restaurant and pub. Dream actually. My Grandpa Shitz was a farmer in the old country. He harvested the freshest ingredients and always said that quality is the top priority. Point and case, if a blueberry didn't pass his strict guidelines, he would simply pick it, and toss it into the sea. Every peacock, every bluegill, everything had to pass his quality control. He said that people eat food, and that food should taste good. I really agree with that philosophy. Don't you?" asked Chef Will.

"That's a pretty obvious statement, but I suppose I agree," said First Lieutenant.

"Yeah, I mean my Grandpa Shitz was a smart man. He died when I was very young, but I always wanted to honor him by opening a restaurant in his name. Will-Shitz Pub. That has a nice ring, doesn't it?" asked Chef Will.

"Yeah, I suppose. Listen. I'd love to sit around and reminisce about your Grandpa Shitz, but you see those guards? We're running out of time. If we're going to execute Project Save First Lieutenant, we have to do it now. "

"Fine," said Chef Will. "But if I'm going to be a part of this, I want my name on the project too."

"You got it. I'll rename the operation to Operation Save First Lieutenant and Chef Will," said First Lieutenant.

"I asked you to perform two very simple tasks," The Queen Mary said with authority in her voice. "Catch and kill an easy baker's dozen blue whales, and on your way home, stop and get a shipment of blueberry jam. Yet, you insist on failing at your tasks. Your excuses are boring to me. I get sick. I can't see. Whales hate me. Blueberry jam is sticky."

"Well it is," interrupted Captain Limb.

"Silence. When I'm speaking words, you are to listen. I am very disappointed in your whole crew. I have no choice but to detain all of you. Guards take them," said The Queen Mary only to be interrupted by First Lieutenant yelling: "Fire at Will," The deckhands scampered about to each of their cannons, cheering and rejoicing in glee. Out towards the middle of the harbor stood Chef Will standing firm in the Cog's only dingy. The first cannon exploded with a loud boom, followed by the second, third and fourth.

"What is this?" The Queen Mary bellowed. "Who is firing those cannons?"

"It appears to be the deckhands. They are firing at that chef standing in a dingy in the harbor. Woah. They are getting really close. This certainly is very amusing" said one of the guards as he began to laugh and cheer.

"Woah. They nearly missed that chef. This is entertaining," laughed The Queen Mary. "Look at how scared that chef is in that dingy. Those cannonballs are whizzing right by his head."

"Keep firing. Straight and near," yelled First Lieutenant. Carefully stepping over the edge of the rail, he grabbed a nearby rope and began to lower himself in the water. As his feet touched the cold icy sea, he soon realized that the water itself was fairly uncomfortable.

"Oh. This water is cold. I can't stop now. Operation Save First Lieutenant and Chef Will must go on," He carefully lowered his body into the icy water and began to slowly dog paddle swim his way over to the dingy. He carefully navigated the cannon ball splashes to make sure he wasn't hit by any incoming cannon ball rounds. Arriving at the dingy, First Lieutenant grabbed the side. "First Lieutenant. Am I glad to see you," yelled Chef Will.

"Now's our chance. Hop in the water with me and we'll swim away while no one is looking," First Lieutenant said. "I can't swim," said Chef Will

"What? You can't swim? Don't you think you should have said something before we started this plan?" asked First Lieutenant.

"I didn't think it would be an issue," said Chef Will.

"What the hell are we going to do now?" said First Lieutenant as he gazed around.

"You know. There's a ton of cannon smoke. I can barely see The Queen Mary, the Cog at this point. What if we simply cut the rope and row away to safety?" said Chef Will.

"That's not a terrible idea. Do you have a knife?" asked First Lieutenant.

"I sure do. It's in my galley, next to my cleaver on The Queen Mary, The Cog," said Chef Will.

"Alright. I'll dog paddle swim back to the Cog, grab the knife, dog paddle swim back, and we'll cut the rope," said First Lieutenant.

"Great plan. I'll keep standing here and let these moronic deckhands use me as target practice. See you in a bit." said Chef Will.

First Lieutenant began his dog paddle swim back to The Queen Mary, the Cog with cannonballs still splashing around him. The noise was deafening from all the cannons still firing at Will. Finally, after several minutes of dog paddle swimming back, First Lieutenant reached the rope ladder. He climbed up the side of the cog and was greeted by a deckhand who helped him over the rail.

"How was your swim?" the deckhand asked. "Oh. Well. It was refreshing," said First Lieutenant. "If you'll excuse me, I need to go get something." First Lieutenant ran towards the rear of the cog being careful not to get noticed by The Queen Mary who was still laughing and giggling at Chef Will. First Lieutenant arrived at the back of the Cog and proceeded down the stairs towards the galley. Finally arriving at the galley, he thought to himself. "Now why did I come down here?" First Lieutenant thought for a second. He couldn't remember why he was down in the galley for the life of him. Damn it. This always happens, he thought.

"Well. I'm not going to waste any time standing here. I need to get back to Chef Will," he said out loud.

"You bastards. Go ahead. Keep firing. You'll be sorry," Chef Will screamed as some of the cannonballs started to get closer.

"Me thinks we're getting closer," said one of the deckhands.

"What are those? Seven pounders? Those cannonballs are weak," screamed Chef Will now spotting First Lieutenant dog paddle swimming back to him. "Go ahead. Why don't you fire your cannonballs faster. I can take it," said Chef Will. "You're back. Did you find my knife?" asked Chef Will.

"Damn it. That was the reason I went back to the galley. I KNEW I went there for a reason. I guess I'll have to swim back.

Do you have anything to write with? I need to make myself a note," said First Lieutenant.

"You know. That might not be necessary. It looks like the rope is just tied to the dingy using a sailor's knot. Do you know how to untie those?" asked Chef Will.

"Wait. I surely do. Help me in the dingy. This water is freezing," said First Lieutenant. Chef Will grabbed First Lieutenant by his britches and hoisted him aboard the dingy. The whole harbor was now filled with thick cannon smoke. "Now's our chance. Let me untie this knot, and we'll row away. Head towards that buttery. We'll hide there," said First Lieutenant.

"The what?" asked Chef Will.

"The buttery. The place where they make butter! You can see it on shore with the red roof. I think we should try and hide somewhere where no one will think to look for us!" said First Lieutenant as he untied the knot with a simple tug. They slowly rowed away amongst the smoke towards the shore.

"Me can't see a bloody thing," said one of the deckhands aiming into a cloud of cannon smoke.

"I either," said another.

"Should we keep firing?" another deckhand screamed.

"First Lieutenant didn't tell us to stop. Me thinks we should keep firing until we run out of cannonballs," said another deckhand down the line of cannons.

The Queen Mary still on the dock laughed and giggled out loud. "I'm giggling out loud," she said. "My this is very entertaining. I love a great display of force towards insignificant people," the Queen Mary said. "All this is well and good. But I insist we stop, Captain Limb. Do we really need this exercise to continue?" she asked.

I never ordered the exercise to begin with, he thought. "Sure, Cease fire. Cease fire," Captain Limb yelled out. "Pull in Will." The deckhands grabbed the line and began to pull.

"Will's lost weight," one deckhand noticed.

"Significant," yelled another. The deckhands pulled and pulled and finally reached the end of the rope.

"Where's Chef Will?" one deckhand said.

"Me thinks we sank him. There's no dingy either. Did we actually hit him this time?" asked another deckhand.

"Me thinks we did. Three cheers. Three cheers for us," said a deckhand down the line of cannons. "Hip, hip, hip," they yelled.

"What's for dinner?" asked another deckhand. "Did Chef Will freeze anything by any chance with instructions on how to reheat?" asked another.

"Captain Limb. I sincerely appreciate the cannon demonstration, but it doesn't change the fact that you failed me in every way," said The Queen Mary. "You really leave me no choice. No choice at all."

"Let me explain," interrupted Captain Limb. "As we all know, whales are moronic beasts. It's not my fault they never appeared out of the sea. As far as the blueberry jam. First Lieutenant is at fault for that,"

"Where is he?" interrupted The Queen Mary.

"I'm not entirely sure," said Captain Limb.

"No matter. I feel you are all responsible for this disaster. You, First Lieutenant, and your crew have ruined my day. Possibly my whole week. Maybe even my whole year. I am The Queen Mary. Divine. Guards, please assemble and gather everyone to be sent to the castle dungeon for processing," The Queen Mary's guards formed a line and began to collect deckhands for processing.

"Single File. Please remain calm. You are in good hands," yelled the guards.

"Speaking of hands, make sure you self-shackle to the deckhand in front of you. Thank you for your cooperation." The deckhands all lined up with Captain Limb leading the front of the chain gang.

"Forward," the guards yelled and the crew of The Queen Mary, the Cog, marched towards the castle dungeon.

Chapter Ten

Judgement Hour Day

"That tickles," Margarine said to Vole who was scampering across her feet. "You know how ticklish my feet are. Knock it off," she scolded. "Today's going to be a busy day. It's Thursday," she said. Thursday was one of The Queen Mary's favorite days of the week. Every Thursday was Judgement hour where she was responsible for holding high court. She would bring each of the prisoners up from the castle dungeon and sentence them for their misdeeds. It was going to be a pretty busy Judgement hour considering the recent incarcerations of all the crew of The Queen Mary, The Cog. "Today, The Queen Mary is going to want to look her very best while she sentences simpletons. I think a long-tailed gown will be the way to go. Especially something that breathes easy. It might be a very long day if she decides to hear everyone's story,"

"Margarine. Do you have my attire ready?" yelled The Queen Mary.

"I certainly have. I picked a lovely gown today. Very breathable," said Margarine.

"Good. I have a full docket of people I need to sentence today. It's going to be a very busy day and I want to look my very best," The Queen Mary slipped into her gown and slipped her peacock feathered shoes on. "It's going to be a lot of fun guiding simpletons towards goals by punishment. Oh, how I simply love Thursdays," yelled The Queen Mary spinning around in glee.

It was a beautiful Thursday morning in Blueburrie. Two peacocks were perched high on the city wall, cackling a morning song.

"Ray, Ray, wake up. It's Thursday. It's judgement hour day." said Flounder. Ray sat in his queen size bunk and rubbed his eyes.

"I sometimes get so warm at night with these down comforters," Ray said.

"I can't get used to the peacock silk sheets. They're so slippery. I often slide right out of bed," said Flounder.

"I just want to go home to my own bed. Who can live like this?" said Ray.

"These conditions are unaccepted. Should we wake Mrs. Warwick?" asked Flounder.

"Let her sleep. It's only 9:30am," said Ray. The two acquaintances sat silent looking out the window.

Two guards opened the cell door and announced their presence. "We're here. We want you to listen," they said with a firm sound in their voices. "Today, is Thursday. Judgement hour day. You have been ordered to the grand hall where The Queen Mary will hold court. The people you will witness are real. They are not actors. They are actual simpletons with real offences. By becoming a prisoner in our dungeon, you have agreed to drop your claims and have your disputes settled there, in our forum. The Queen Mary's Court," said the two guards in unison. Mrs. Warwick suddenly awoke.

"Can't you people keep it down? You scared me half to death and back. Now, what were you saying about actors? Are we going to be in some sort of play?" ask Mrs. Warwick.

"No Ma'am. The people you will see in the grand hall are not actors. They are real people," said the guard.

"Oh. I see. I was going to say, I don't know if I'm fond of taking part in any type of play. I'm not fond of balls, and plays. Just too old I guess," Mrs. Warwick said.

"I like plays and balls," said Flounder.

"I know, as you should. You're a young man with the whole world in front of you. Granted you're a prisoner in this dungeon, but soon enough you may be a free man," said Mrs. Warwick.

"I hope so. Living here is insufferable," said Flounder.

Down in the grand hall, Papa Tomkins, The Queen Mary's trusted city clerk was preparing for the day. He had a stack of court orders that were ready to be processed. "Woof. This is going to be a pretty busy day," he said thumbing through some of the papers. "A dog is a man's best friend," he said to himself while organizing the stack. Papa was once voted the town's friendliest man, and would often treat people with common inspirational quotes, that didn't always apply to the situation at hand.

"Papa. Going to be a busy day?" asked one of the townspeople.

"Busier than yesterday. A rising tide lifts all boats," he said while walking to the courtyard. On the stage, behind a large desk sat The Queen Mary. A crowd of townspeople had gathered around the center stage. Behind the stage prisoners were lined up waiting their turn for sentencing. Papa Tomkins gathered his things and headed to the podium.

"Now calling to order. Case number XXXVI The Queen Mary verses Hu. How do you plead?"

"Mostly Not -Guilty," yelled Hu.

"Hu, you were brought here today for offending The Queen Mary by presenting mushy roasted peacock. As we all know, nothing tastes more offensive than mushy peacock bones. On the night of the ball, we were all looking forward to tasty roasted and perfectly juiced peacock. Although the bird was perfectly juiced, for some reason The Queen Mary herself bit down on a mushy bone. This is a punishable offense," said Papa.

"I understand. I'm pleading mostly not- guilty because I wasn't the one who actually juiced the cock that night. I'm not even sure who did it," said Hu.

"Being stupid is not an excuse," said The Queen Mary. "I sentence you to 21 months in dungeon level 11," said The Queen

Mary. Hu sighed and left the stage wondering if his dream of ever owning his own butcher shop would ever come true.

Papa grabbed the next paper off the pile and read out loud. "Now calling case number XXXVII. The Queen Mary verses Mrs. Warwick. How do you plead?"

"What do you mean by plead?" said Mrs. Warwick.

"Do you think you were guilty or not guilty?" asked Papa.

"Oh. I'm guilty. I didn't disperse," said Mrs. Warwick.

"You understand, when I travel I am so important I cannot stop. I have told the simpletons of Blueburrie over and over and over I stop for no one. Mrs. Warwick, I must make an example of you. I sentence you to 22 months in dungeon level 3," said The Queen Mary.

Mrs. Warwick sighed and left the stage. Well. I suppose my cat is going to die. No one home to feed him. Guess I'll get another cat, she thought.

"This is terribly fun. I am experiencing so much joy saving people's lives by discipline," The Queen Mary said out loud. She looked over at Papa Tomkins who was preparing the next case. "Papa Tomkins, Papa Tomkins," she yelled as she gave him a thumbs up. Papa looked back, smiled, and gave a thumbs up back.

"Now calling to order. Case Number XXXVIII. The Queen Mary verses Pom and Gil for sun-kissed blueberries. How do you plead?" asked Papa.

"Not Guilty. Well, not applicable rather," said Pom.

"Not applicable?"

"Yes, non-applicable. Our blueberries are sun-dried every year. We take great pride in making sure that each blueberry is sun-dried to The Queen Mary's level of quality. Every morning we rotate each berry counter clockwise, one quarter turn. We repeat the process ever fifteen minutes, rotating the berry another quarter turn. This results in a perfectly sun-dried berry. At no time do we allow the berry to be sun-kissed," said Pom.

"All's I know is that the blueberry I bit in to was not even close to being dry. It tasted funny. Like it was sun-kissed," said The Queen Mary.

"Are you sure it was one of my blueberries?" asked Pom

"I'm nearly positive. I must say, Pom, I'm very upset you would have the gall to ask me a question. For I am divine. All the words that flow from my mouth are chosen very carefully by my brain, directly placed there by the Almighty," said The Queen Mary, her voice starting to get angrier.

"I didn't."

"You didn't. That's right, you didn't. You didn't think. That's your problem. You fed me a sun-kissed blueberry and quite honestly, I'm offended that you would do such a thing on purpose," The Queen Mary now began to get even more frustrated and angry. The veins in her neck and calves started to protrude as her face began to change to a darker shade of red. "For offending The Queen Mary, I sentence you to 87 months in dungeon level 2," she screamed. "Guards, take him away."

Papa licked his thumb and grabbed the next summons in his pile of papers. "A bluebird in the hand is worth two in the bush," he said quietly to some townspeople around him. They looked at him with a confused gaze in their eyes. One of the townspeople slowly gave him a thumbs up, just so Papa Tompkins' awkward stare would stop. "Now calling case number XXXVIIII. The Queen Mary verses Gil. How do you plead?"

Before Gil could answer The Queen Mary interrupted. "I'll tell you how he pleads. Guilty. Guilty by association. Gil, I sentence you to 23 months in dungeon level 2. One more day than your simpleton acquaintance. Maybe this will teach you to associate with simpletons like Pom. Guards take him away," The Queen Mary yelled. "Papa. Who's next?"

"Almighty Damned. This is going to be a big one. Now calling The Queen Mary verses the whole crew of The Queen Mary, the Cog," said Papa. The townspeople gasped as a long line of deckhands walked single file throughout the crowd. "Please excuse how some of us are walking. We haven't had time to get our land legs yet," said one of the deckhands to Papa. Two single lines of 20 deckhands stood at attention with Captain Limb front and center. "For violating The Queen Mary's orders you have been brought here today to explain why the town has no delicious blue whale meat, and no sweet, sweet, delicious blueberry jam. I like to spread my jam on toast. And my favorite part of the blue whale is the median notch. So tasty. I was so looking forward to these sweet treats. You failed us. You failed the whole town of Blueburrie," said The Queen Mary.

"Whales hate me," said Captain Limb.

"Whales have no feelings. They are moronic beasts," yelled The Queen Mary.

"Yes, they are moronic, but they also no longer exist. We sailed for several months, never spotting a single whale," said Captain Limb.

"Whales are huge. I find it hard to believe that you couldn't spot a single whale. You certainly have placed me in quite a predicament. I want to believe you, but I feel that you are incapable of doing your job. I also feel that your deckhands should suffer the same punishment simply because they followed your orders," said The Queen Mary.

"Did you enjoy the cannon demonstration?" asked Captain Limb.

"Yes. It was near divine. I do appreciate that, but I feel like you were trying to distract me. This is very unfortunate. I need to sentence you and your crew. I will go light and sentence you to 21 months in dungeon level 4. Guards, take them away."

"Busy, busy, busy," Papa Tomkins sang to himself as he thumbed through his papers. "Oh, last one of the day. Ray Ferch, Tap Dancer," he said, pausing for a second to remember why he despised tappers. Several years earlier, Papa was out gardening blueberries when a group of tapper thugs approached him. Unlike Ray, they used their tap-dancing abilities in a negative way. They circled him, began to snap their fingers, and went into a step-heel and heel-step routine. The tapper thugs laughed and ridiculed Papa, calling him beat-deaf. Curling into the fetal position, Papa cried and cried until the thugs left him alone. It was fairly well known that there was a gang of rough neck tappers in Blueburrie. They would use their tap dancing to influence and harass townspeople. Most knew they usually never meant any harm, but if you heard them tapping towards you it was best to get out of the way. Unfortunately, Papa, wasn't so lucky that day and he received the full brunt of a step-heel, heel-step attack. He was never the same after that day.

"Now calling to order. The Queen Mary verses Ray McJohnson and Flounder Crotx, for disappointing and ruining a ball in honor of The Queen Mary's new friends. How do you plead?" Ray and Flounder stood in silence staring at Papa. "How do you plead?" he asked again.

"Oh. Are you talking to us?" asked Ray

"Yes, your dreaded tap dancing. How do you plead for the incident at the ball?" yelled Papa.

"Yes," responded Flounder.

"No," responded Ray

"What are you two? Simpletons? How do you plead?" yelled Papa.

"Yes," responded Flounder.

"Yes," responded Ray.

"Yes to what? What the hell are you two talking about? Are you guilty or not guilty?" Papa screamed in anger.

"Oh. I guess we're both? It's really hard to say," said Ray.

"Ray, I think you're right. We're definitely both," agreed Flounder.

"Obviously, you two are incapable of thinking. Please address The Queen Mary and state your story."

Ray looked up at The Queen Mary who sat high on a stage above him. "Your majestic majesty. As you know, my name is Ray McJohnson. I was born a poor simpleton in this lovely, safe, town known as Blueburrie. My whole life I found music to be magical and special. No matter what tune I heard, or hummed, or sang I could instantly find the beat. My big toe would start tapping and my heart would race and my brain would say 'Dance.' It wasn't until I was nearly three years old that I decided to be a full time tap dancer. I begged my mother and father for lessons. I would stay awake at night secretly snapping my fingers to made up songs in my head. When I was 11 years old, I found two wooden planks while playing down by the harbor one day. I strapped the planks to my feet and noticed that when I tapped them a beautiful clacking sound was produced. I loved my plank shoes for many, many years and I practiced every day. It wasn't until my best acquaintance, Flounder bought me my pair of tappers on my thirteenth birthday. He saved every piloncito he ever earned to get me my tappers. The day I slide those comfortable beauties on I was unstoppable. My paradiddle couldn't be stopped. Shirley temples were seamless. My stamp steel heel turns? Not even a slight concern. All because of my shoes, and my best acquaintance, Flounder Crotx," said Ray.

"I like Ray's clacking, what can I say? It makes me feel good inside," said Flounder.

"That's such a great point, Flounder," said Ray "I want to make everyone feel good when I tap. Sure, I love the sound myself, but I know it brings so much joy to everyone around me. That's why I constantly wear my shoes and protect them with my life," said Ray.

"He does love those shoes. So do I. At night, while Ray is often sleeping, I will sneak in his bedroom and shine his tapper shoes so they look nice and pristine," said Flounder.

"That was you?" said Ray.

"Oh, you bet. I get nervous sometimes because I know you like to wear your tapper shoes to bed and I don't want to wake you," said Flounder.

"Enough," yelled The Queen Mary. "This isn't some forum for you two simpletons to talk about old times and play grab ass. You were brought here today because your tap-dancing presentation was dare I say, abominable. Abominable and atrocious. I was hardly satisfied, and I know that all of my friends of Blueburrie feel the same way. You brought shame to our townspeople. I suspect it was because you were too busy drinking at NumNuks with Mrs. Warwick. But since I wasn't invited how the fuck would I know?" The townspeople gasped as it was very rare for The Queen Mary to use 20th century curse words. Clearly, she was upset about not being invited.

"Your majestic majesty. We would have invited you. The problem is, I have no way to contact you. You have never associated with simpletons. We didn't think we were worthy of your presence in close spaces," said Ray.

"You're stupid. And you're right, you are a simpleton. Your inability to amuse has caused me to become irrational. For denying myself and the townspeople the right to a good show of tap dancing, I demand you take off your tappers and throw them in the community pond," said The Queen Mary.

"What? My tappers? You mean my tap shoes?" cried Ray.

"The very same. I demand you remove them at once and toss them in, never to be seen again," she yelled.

"But. I need my tappers. If I don't have my tappers how will anyone hear that beautiful tapping sound everyone has come to know and love? Without my tappers, all people will hear is the slapping sound of my bare feet," Ray said as he began to tear up.

"That sounds like a you problem and not a me problem," laughed The Queen Mary. "I sentence you and your dim-witted acquaintance, Flounder to 240 months in dungeon level 3. You'll have plenty of time to paradiddle and slap those feet of yours, while you think about what you've done."

"But," said Flounder.

"But nothing. Guards, remove Ray's tappers and throw them in the community pond. Once complete. Take them away."

"My tappers," cried Ray.

"Ray, stay vigorous," screamed Flounder.

Chapter Eleven

THE PLAN

Hiding in a haystack near the harbor, Chef Will and First Lieutenant peaked through and noticed that no guards were in sight.

"We've been hiding here for over two hours. Do you think it's safe to leave?" asked Chef Will.

"I think we better think about moving soon. A half hour ago when that donkey came to graze, he nearly bit my crotch," said First Lieutenant.

"I was bit by a donkey once, they're dangerous," said Chef Will.

"No kidding. How did that happen?" asked First Lieutenant.

"Same situation. I was hiding in a haystack and a random donkey came up to graze. He bit me pretty bad in my abdomen," said Chef Will.

"Danger is always lurking that's for sure. I think we have a pretty good chance to run for that buttery, and hide there overnight," said First Lieutenant.

"Buttery? Don't you mean creamery?" asked Chef Will.

"No, the buttery. The place where they make butter," said First Lieutenant.

"I think it's a creamery. A buttery is a place where food and drinks specifically wine and liquor are stored. Similar to a pantry," said Chef Will.

"I think you're wrong. I'm almost positive it's called a buttery. It doesn't matter. Let's head for that red roofed building and hide there. Any place is better than this haystack," said First Lieutenant.

"Let's do this," yelled Chef Will as they sprang from the haystack and ran as fast as they could for the back door of the buttery.

First Lieutenant grabbed the door handle and tried to turn it. "It's locked," he whispered.

"That figures. Should we head back to our haystack?" asked Chef Will in a panic.

"No. Let's try to bust the door down. On twelve. One, Two, Three, Four," whispered First Lieutenant.

"Wait. Should we try and bust the door down on twelve or say twelve and then bust the door down?" asked Chef Will.

"When I say twelve, we bust. Ready? One, two, three, four, five, six, seven--."

"Wait. I think I heard something," said Chef Will. The two paused and looked around. The silence was broken by a peahen walking by the door.

"Oh. It was just a peahen. Never mind," said Chef Will.

"Ready?" asked First Lieutenant.

"Ready." "One, two, three, four, five, six, seven, nine."

"Wait," interrupted Chef Will. "What happened to eight?"

"What?" asked First Lieutenant. "What happened to eight? You skipped eight,"

"I did?" asked First Lieutenant.

"Yeah, you said, 'five, six, seven, nine,' but no eight," said Chef Will.

"I don't think this is going to work. We need another plan," said First Lieutenant. The two paused and looked around to try and figure out a different plan.

"When you turned the door handle, which way did you turn it?" asked Chef Will.

"The way I always turn door handles, counter-clockwise," said First Lieutenant. "Counter? Counter-clockwise? You never turn a door handle that way," said Chef Will.

"That's the way I was taught," said First Lieutenant.

"Well, it's not right," Chef Will grabs the door handle and turns clockwise opening the door. "See," said Chef Will

"Ah, you two must be my new interns, welcome to my creamery called the buttery," said Kent.

"Who us?" asked First Lieutenant.

"Yes, of course. I sent a jay a few weeks ago to The Queen Mary expressing my concerns. This is really perfect timing. The butter in vat 4 is just about ready to churn. Grab those scotch hands and come join me," said Kent. The two looked at each other with confusion. First Lieutenant grabbed Chef Will's hands and asked, "These hands?"

"What? No. Those wooden boards over there. The scotch hands," said Kent.

"Oh, I was going to say, I'm not scotch, I'm Roman, with ten percent Dutch," said Chef Will.

"So what made you two decide to get into butter making?" asked Kent.

"Well. Uh. Well," Chef Will began to stutter.

"We decided a few years ago. We met recently and butter has always been our passion," said First Lieutenant.

"Great. We could also use some more passionate buttermen around here. So many people join this profession half assed. It's good to hear someone is passionate."

"That's us. We love the taste, the smell, the feel of butter that's for sure," said First Lieutenant.

"I like to cook with it," said Chef Will. "Cook? Never thought to use butter that way," said Kent.

"Oh, cook? I mean, well I'd like to cook with it someday. I'm not a cook. I don't bake. I surely have never worked on a Cog before," said Chef Will.

Realizing that Chef Will was about to blow their cover, First Lieutenant interrupted, "Well, we're just happy to be here. Thanks for the opportunity."

Kent grabbed his plumper and began to stir. "I'm just really glad for the help. The dungeon is getting so full of prisoners, we really need to increase our supply of butter for all the lobster they feed those criminals."

"You know they're not all criminals," said First Lieutenant.

"What?" asked Kent, surprised by First Lieutenant's answer.

"Well, I happen to know some very fine men in that dungeon. I find it hard to believe they're all criminals," said First Lieutenant.

"That's probably true," said Kent. "There's a lot of people that reside in that castle, my daughter herself works for The Queen Mary. I had always wished she would work with me as a butterwoman, but it was all for not. When she was very young at her new friendship ball, The Queen Mary took a liking to her and called upon her to be her personal assistant. I must say, I am very proud of her, but I often miss seeing or talking to her," said Kent.

"The Queen Mary doesn't allow her to visit?" asked First Lieutenant.

"Never. She's much too important to allow her to leave. It saddens me that Margarine can't visit, but I know deep in my heart that she's happy and blessed," said Kent. "Now, how about we get some of this churned butter in to stick form? It's really the most exciting part," said Kent.

****

"Proceed single file. Prisoners move forward," yelled one of the guards as they began to file away the recently sentenced prisoners from judgement hour. "Open cell door 50, Ray Mcdonald, Flounder Crotx, and Paul Warwick enter your cell," yelled the guard.

"Mrs. Warwick. Your name is Paul?" asked Flounder.

"My name is Paula, but close enough," said Mrs. Warwick with a sigh.

"I was going to say. You don't look like a Paul," said Flounder. Ray walked in completely silent behind Flounder.

"Ray, you startled me. I could barely hear you."

"No one can. There's no tapping. There's no clacking. Only slapping. Slapping of my stupid feet," said Ray.

"Now come on, Ray. Your feet don't sound that bad," said Flounder.

"Yes they do. My feet sound like two peacocks fucking," yelled Ray.

"That's not true. I've seen peacocks make love. It doesn't sound like your feet at all," said Flounder.

"I'm just not sure of anything anymore. This place is so depressing. I try to bring joy and happiness with my tap dancing and what thanks do I get? The Queen Mary rips my tap dance shoes off my feet and throws them in to the community pond," said Ray.

"Do you think they float?" asked Flounder.

"I doubt it. They're peacock skin. Peacocks don't swim. Chances are those tappers are long gone. At the bottom of the community pond, with all the dreams The Queen Mary has ruined," said Ray.

"Ray, I don't like your despondency. It's not the Ray I know. You are a dreamer, and you bring joy. These questions you raise. They concern me," said Flounder.

"Flounder, look at my feet. They're as disgusting as yours. All's I'm saying is that maybe this isn't the right place for me. For you. For us," said Ray.

"I agree with you," said Mrs. Warwick. "It really upsets me that the guards can't even get my name right."

"You think there's a chance we could break out of this place? Break out of this town?" said Ray.

"Are you crazy?" both Flounder and Mrs. Warwick said in unison.

"I'm hardly crazy. I've just been thinking lately. After talking with my cousin Toss, he gets to experience so many things. Sure, it's dangerous. Sure, there are animals waiting to kill you. Sure, there's mold. But, are we living?" said Ray.

"Maybe I could get you another pair of tappers and you could show your tap dancing to people on the other side of this flat earth?" said Flounder.

"Exactly. If you got me new tappers, I could spread tap love on this planet just like you spread blueberry jelly on toast," said Ray.

"You boys sure are hopeful. But I honestly think you're crazy," said Mrs. Warwick. "You know my husband, Professor Warwick, studied the outside world for years. He wrote journals about every danger there was and a corresponding solution to each. He found so many dangers that he was able to document. Mold, rats, prickly plants, he called 'ouchers.' Fish that fly, flies that bite, fallen trees, mean bears, eye level twigs on trees. Just talking about the findings alone makes me anxious," said Mrs. Warwick.

"These journals. Do you still have them?" asked Ray.

"Of course. Not with me, but they're in Professor Warwick's den. Why do you ask?"

"Are you thinking what I'm thinking Flounder?" asked Ray.

"We should borrow the journals, read them, and increase our level of anxiety too?" said Flounder.

"No. We borrow the journals. We read them. We learn about dangers, and remember the solutions. Then, we bust out of this almighty forsaken place and leave the city and live. Live damn it," said Ray.

"I admire your ideas. You can borrow my journals if we ever get out of here," said Mrs. Warwick

"I'm in. I'll follow you anywhere," said Flounder.

"Then the plan is set. But we're going to need help," said Ray.

Chapter Twelve

OPERATION L.E.A.F.

❧

"Inspection time. Please stand and place your arms to your sides and make sure your feet are parallel with the ground," the guard said as they entered Porksmu's cell.

"Looks like you've been busy again with your silly inventions. What is this some type of blending machine?" asked the Guard.

"It's called a stirmaker. I plan on putting different ingredients in it someday and hopefully this machine will mix them all together by itself," said Porksmu. The guards all began to chuckle as they pulled items off shelves, searched boxes, and tore designs off the walls.

"The Queen Mary appreciates the fact that I take the extra time to tear paintings and artwork off the walls. She seems to think that it's the number one way prisoners escape is by making holes in walls and covering them up with artwork," said the guard.

"I wouldn't know anything about that," said Porksmu.

"Of course, you wouldn't. You're a simpleton," laughed the guard. "Where's your bed?" asked the guard.

"I converted it to a dining set. Complete with four chairs," said Porksmu.

"Expecting guests? Everything looks clear here. No violations. But to keep your creativity in check, guards, take away three of the four chairs from the dining set. I wouldn't want him to have any bright ideas and invite fellow prisoners over for a dinner party," laughed the guard.

The cell doors slammed shut and Porksmu cursed under his breath. "Wouldn't want you to have any dinner parties. What an asshole. I'll show them," Porksmu pushed in his only chair and began to organize the mess the guards left behind. "Meow," said Mr. Wriggly who appeared at the window.

"I know. What a mess. The guards really did a number this time," said Porksmu.

"Meow, meow."

"I agree. The guards are certainly unjust in many ways. What difference does it make if I invent items that make my life here in the dungeon a little more tolerable," said Porksmu.

"Meow," said Mr. Wriggly.

"Ha. You're right. Those dining chairs will probably break as soon as those guard's fat asses sit on them," laughed Porksmu.

****

"Help me push this Spanish donkey out of the way," Pom said to Gil.

"Why is this thing even in our cell?" asked Gil.

"Who knows. I heard some rumors The Queen Mary was remodeling the torture chamber and they needed to put this somewhere," said Pom.

"Figures it would be our cell. That's just the luck we've been having lately. I'm still not exactly sure why I'm even here. I didn't have anything to do with your sun-kissed blueberries," said Gil.

"I'm pretty sure I told you they were going to get sun-kissed if you left them out too long. Didn't I tell you that?" asked Gil.

"I can't remember. You may have said something to that effect," said Pom.

"I certainly did. I told you at least 54 times," said Gil.

"Well, there's nothing we can really do about it now. We're both stuck in here," said Pom.

"We're stuck in here all right. But just so you are aware, it's not my fault. I told you about the sun-kissing."

"Yeah I know, I know," said Pom.

"Do you know what's for dinner?" asked Gil.

"Crab Legs, I heard," said Pom.

"Almighty. Now we're being forced to eat legs," sighed Gil.

****

"Quit pushing. Me's barely got room to move in here," yelled one of the deckhands.

"Me was here first. This is my sleeping pad," yelled one of the deckhands.

"Twenty deckhands in two cells. It's just not right," said Dr. Dunston. "If my calculations are correct there should only be a maximum of four and a half prisoners per each cell. We've got twenty-one people in this cell including me. I understand overcrowding is an issue, but this is a little ridiculous. In these living conditions it'll be a miracle if we all don't catch yeast infections," said Dr. Dunston.

"Dr. Dunston, Dr. Dunston," whispered a deckhand, pushing others aside to talk to him.

"If it isn't my favorite deckhand. How are you feeling? How is your finger? Still sore?" asked Dr Dunston.

"Me finger feels fine."

"How's the chest? Still on fire from that medication I gave you?"

"No, me chest is fine too. Very tolerable temperature it seems," said the deckhand.

"That's great to hear. You're really a miracle patient of mine. Most people experience that burning for months, if not, years. And your maxillary teeth. Let's take a peek at that. Seems fine. Looks like you're in great health," said Dr. Dunston.

"Well, not exactly. Me's got this rash on my side," said the deckhand.

"Well, let's take a look," as he lifted the deckhand's shirt to inspect the rash. "Oh, what the hell. You've got a yeast infection. I knew it. I said it two minutes ago. You better stay clear and sit in that corner by yourself. Almighty damned if we don't all catch this now," said the doctor as he washed his hands in a puddle that was on the cell floor. "We gotta get out of here," said Dr. Dunston.

****

Hu gazed out his window looking at the sun starting to set over the horizon. He could smell the sweet smell of roasting peacock occasionally through the crack in his window. Smells like my Uncle Blur is roasting one hell of a bird. Smells like a twenty-eight pounder, he thought to himself.

"You've tasted peacock before?" asked a mysterious girl lurking in the shadows.

"Tasted it? I cook it nearly every day. My uncle owns Blur's Butcher Shoppe. I'm Hu, his nephew," said Hu.

"My name is Apricot, but my acquaintances call me Ape," the girl said as she appeared out of the shadows.

"Yikes. I didn't even know you were here," said Hu.

"Most don't. I'm pretty sly. I like to lurk in the shadows and hide most of the time. I'm pretty silent too. Sometimes I go days without ever muttering a single word. But not today. Today I'm being very talkative and not sly at all," said Ape.

"Good thing. I could really use the company. I'm really excited you're here. Speaking of. Why are you here?" asked Hu.

"Indecisiveness," said Ape. "I was out picking blueberries one day and The Queen Mary approached me. She asked if I would rather spend six days on moon, or twenty-five days on the sun. She caught me totally off guard. I didn't know how to answer. By the time I could state my opinion, she yelled for the guards and placed me in this dungeon for being indecisive. I was four years old," said Ape.

"Four years old? You must be in your twenties. How long have you been trapped here?" asked Hu.

"A long time. I feel like I've missed most of my childhood, teenage years, and my early twenties," said Ape.

"You certainly have. How could The Queen Mary sentence you for that long?" asked Hu.

"On judgement hour day I was so nervous. She asked me the question again and I froze. I had the answer I wanted to give, but her divineness simply overtook me. I sat there frozen, quiet, like a vole. Didn't say a word. That really angered her. She told me that if I couldn't answer a simple question like would I rather spend six days on the moon or twenty-five days on the sun, how would I be able to be a productive member of Blueburrie? She said that I should spend the rest of my life here. She was right. I deserved the sentence I got," said Ape.

"Are you crazy? You were four years old. I'm twenty-four years old, and I'm not even sure how to answer that question. You don't deserve to be here. You deserve to be free," said Hu.

"I do? But I'm an old ugly hag. No one would want to be with me," said Ape.

"That is not true, Ape. You are not ugly. You are certainly not a hag. You are a beautiful woman. I honestly suspect that The Queen Mary was threatened by your beauty and that's the real reason she threw you in this dungeon."

Ape began to cry. She had never felt so appreciated. She stood and walked over to Hu and whispered. "I know we're not supposed to hug other prisoners, but I don't care," as she gave him an embrace. "If we ever get the chance to get out of here let's do it. Promise me," she said.

"I promise," said Hu.

"Now what's your story. Why are you here, and what do you dream about?" asked Ape.

"You don't happen to have a sister, do you?" asked Hu.

****

"I need order. Order please," yelled Captain Limb to his deckhands. "Please count off. How many of you are here with me?" he asked.

"Me thinks twenty," said one of the deckhands.

"Wonderful, wonderful. Has anyone seen First Lieutenant?" asked Captain Limb. A silence came over the crew as they looked around in their cell.

"Me or me deckhands haven't seen him," one of deckhands said.

"Can any of you give me a status?" asked Captain Limb.

"Status? Me not sure what you mean," asked the deckhand.

"Status. What's the status?" said Captain Limb again. They all simply shrugged and looked at each other.

"Me thinks you're trying to ask us our status?" said the deckhand.

"Yes, that's correct. What is your status?" asked Captain Limb.

"Well. We're in this prisoner cell in the dungeon," said the deckhand.

"Ah. Wonderful. Thank you. Now. We are stuck here aren't we. This is quite the situation," said Captain Limb.

"Me thinks the deckhands are small enough to squeeze through that window," said one of the deckhands.

"Ah. Wonderful. Yes. The window. That seems like a valuable option. You say that the deckhands are small enough?" asked Captain Limb.

"Yes. Very small. We're small, but we're very fast and very efficient. We could squeeze through that window and run very quickly down Fourth Avenue to the The Queen Mary, the Cog. Just give the word," said the deckhand with excitement.

"Yes. Very well. Very good idea indeed. Let me think about this. I need a nap. Would it be possible that you round up the deckhands and tell them I need utter silence during my nap? I'll head over that corner now. Remember, silence. Total silence is what I need during my nap," ordered the captain.

"Aye, aye," said the deckhand.

A few cells down a blue jay flew to the window and let out a beautiful jay call.

"Look. It's a new jay. I wonder who it's for," said Mrs. Warwick grabbing the bird by the chest and tearing off the message.

"It's to Ray. It's from his cousin Toss." Ray perked up from his corner and ran over to Mrs. Warwick. "Let me see that," he said, grabbing it from her hand. *Deer Ray. This is your cousin Toss. My ship arrived at the non-believer city of Snurburrie. I left the ship to sight see before my official duties, and did I see some amazing things. There was this dog that could run really fast and jump pretty high. I wondered who the dog belonged to but I never found the owner. I also saw this huge sign that said: "Farmers Market This Way," but I avoided it because I'm not a farmer. I kicked some non-believer in the thigh, and he fell down. He cursed at me, I think. He said something about me being rude, or something. The weather is nice. Not too hot, and not too cold. I think I stepped in some bear shit. At least I think it was bear shit. But actually, come to think of it, it probably was that fast dog's shit. Hope to see you soon. Love, Toss*

"Wow. Your cousin Toss sure is having the time of his life," said Flounder. "Do you think he'll bring you back any souvenirs?"

"Souvenirs?" said Ray. "I don't want souvenirs. See, this is exactly what I'm talking about. We're stuck in here and Toss is out exploring the world. I'm obviously too much of a simpleton to be a dominator, but don't I deserve a life that is exciting like that? Don't we all deserve that? We try our best in life and here we sit. Mrs. Warwick, your cat will probably die. Flounder, your midriff is showing and your feet smell like shit. And me. I couldn't make a tap sound if my life depended on it. No more woe is me's. It's time to start thinking about our plan."

"What plan?" said Flounder.

"What plan? The plan to break out of this dungeon and catch the first ship we can. We're getting out of this town, and we're never looking back," said Ray.

"Oh, yeah, that plan," said Flounder.

"We need a name. Operation. Operation something," said Ray.

"How about Operation Anything?" said Flounder.

"It's too generic. That could mean anything. It has to be more specific," said Ray.

"Operation. . . Escape from this Dungeon in Hopefully Three Weeks' Time?" ask Flounder.

"You're on the right track. That is very specific. My only concern is that when we're casually talking about it, the guards will overhear us and we'll lose the element of surprise," said Ray.

"Operation Leave?" asked Mrs. Warwick.

"Mrs. Warwick, you're a genius. It's short, descriptive, and a perfect name for our plan. Flounder write that down. We've got a lot of work to do getting ready," said Ray.

"Got it, Operation L-E-A-F," said Flounder as he wrote it down on the cell wall.

Chapter Thirteen

SEVERAL WEEKS PASS

Several weeks passed in Blueburrie and the smells of fall filled the air. Peacocks began to grow their winter coats. The bluebirds began to pack and get ready for their journey east. Blue gills began to swim deeper to find refuge from the cold winter ahead. The nightly autumn frosts tickled the blueberry bushes causing them to freeze the sweet berries they produced. Children, those lucky enough to learn to wear footwear, switched from sandals to boots to cover their feet from the autumn chill. The town of Blueburrie was busy, but a sense of loss filled the air. It had been several weeks since The Queen Mary went on a rampage and threw nearly a quarter of the population into the castle dungeon prisoner system. She liked to rave about the program, calling it one of the best in the kingdom, but even still not having people free on the streets of Blueburrie created a burden on the free citizens The Queen Mary called friends.

"I miss my dad sometimes," said Margarine while scratching Hornco's ears. "Every time I take a bite of butter I think of him. I really don't have very many memories, but it sure would be nice to see him again. If only for a few moments. I'd love to tell him about all the good work I'm doing for The Queen Mary. She depends on me so very much. She always tells me how simple I am, but I really believe that without me, she certainly wouldn't have such a divine style," Margarine said. "Do you ever miss your mom or dad?" asked Margarine. Hornco simply looked up at Margarine and shrugged. "I suppose. It's probably pretty tough being a vole.

You probably had lots of brothers and sisters. I don't have any. I'm an only child. At least as far as I know. If I ever meet my dad again, that will be one of the questions I ask him, do I have any siblings. It would be nice to know I suppose," Margarine said while organizing the hairbrushes for The Queen Mary's mid-afternoon hair brushing.

"Margarine, who are you talking to? I told you a million times that vole doesn't understand a damn word you say," said The Queen Mary. "You see him shrugging? He doesn't understand you," yelled The Queen Mary.

"Yes, he does. He shrugs because he doesn't have an opinion. Not because he doesn't understand me," said Margarine.

"Margarine, you are such a simpleton, and no offense, an idiot. That vole is as stupid as you are. No wonder you're acquaintances with that thing. Now where's my brush? Get the one with the peacock eyelashes. I like how soft it feels on my supple hair," said The Queen Mary.

"I don't have any brushes with peacock eyelashes," said Margarine.

"What?"

"I don't have any peacock eyelash brushes," said Margarine.

"I heard you the first time. What do you mean, you don't have any brushes with peacock eyelashes? I specifically told you that I wanted my hair to be brushed with peacock eyelashes," yelled The Queen Mary.

"Well, all I see is either mule or jackass hairbrushes. No peacock eyelash," said Margarine.

"Margarine, you test my patience every day. I simply don't understand why you treat me this way. I really need my hair to be brushed with peacock eyelashes and nothing more, nothing less. Where is Mosh? If someone can get something done around here, it's my number one ball manager, Mosh. Where is he? Someone summon him. I simply must have my eyelashes," yelled The Queen Mary.

Mosh stood on Fourth Avenue staring at the amount of peacock scat that accumulated to well over an inch coating the entire street. "If Suzin thinks I'm going to clean this shit up, he's nuts," Mosh said to himself. "People can barely cross the street without slipping and falling. This just isn't an ascetic thing anymore, this is dangerous," he said out loud. "What in the world have these peacocks been eating," said Mosh before he picked up a piece of peacock scat and smelled it. "Doesn't seem out of the--."

"Is your name, Mosh?" interrupted one of The Queen Mary's guards.

"Yes, yes it is," Mosh responded.

"You have been summoned to The Queen Mary's dressing room," said the guard.

"Is this urgent?" asked Mosh.

"The most urgent. She has requested that you bring a peacock eyelash brush," said the guard.

"Okay. Wait what?" asked Mosh as the guard grabbed his hand and pulled him towards the castle.

"Now presenting: Mosh Wallaces the third," Papa Tomkins announced.

"Wonderful. About time," said The Queen Mary. "Mosh, where were you? I called upon you," asked The Queen Mary.

"I was inspecting Fourth Avenue. It seems to be dangerously full of peacock--."

"Peacocks. Great," interrupted The Queen Mary. "I called upon you because I need as many peacock eye lashes as you can gather. Once you have them collected, I need you to form a hairbrush," said The Queen Mary.

"A hairbrush for the peacocks?" asked Mosh with a confused look on his face.

"No. I want a hairbrush made out of peacock eyelashes for me," she yelled. "What is confusing about that?" she said in a stern voice.

"I'm just not sure I know how to collect peacock eyelashes per se," said Mosh.

"Not sure? Not Sure? Just go and grab a peacock, any peacock will do, hold it by its skinny neck and pluck out a dozen or so of its eyelashes. Seems pretty simple to me," said The Queen Mary.

"I know, but," said Mosh.

"But what? I really don't understand your lack of motivation lately. The fact that you can't gather a mere baker's dozen eyelashes from an incompetent animal infuriates me, Mosh. Ball manager or no ball manager you leave me no choice. You must be taken away," shouted The Queen Mary.

"Do you understand what I do around here? Do you know how many tasks I accomplish?" yelled Mosh as two guards grabbed him and threw his arms behind his back.

"You'll be sorry. Better not plan any balls any time soon. Enjoy juicy peacock? Well not anymore. Bet you a panchereon that you step in some peacock shit on your morning walk," Mosh proclaimed. The guards led Mosh out of the room.

"Guards. Make sure he doesn't get any brunch this morning," The Queen Mary snickered. "Take him away."

****

"Ray, wake up," said Flounder while casually rubbing his shoulder. Ray awoke, confused.

"What day is it?" he said rubbing his eyes.

"It's Thursday. I mean, Monday," said Flounder.

"Well. What day is it?" asked Ray.

"Definitely, Monday. At least, I think. I was never good with day keeping and I failed calendar class in school," said Flounder.

"It doesn't matter. All the days seem to mesh together, honestly. Sure feels cold today. I wonder if autumn is approaching?" asked Ray.

"I think so. A frost covered blueberry rolled into our cell from a nearby blueberry bush the other day. When I bit down, I felt a cold sensation," said Flounder.

"Are you sure it was a blueberry?" asked Ray.

"Pretty sure," said Flounder.

"If autumn is here, winter will be next. We all know that the heat in this dungeon cell barely works. We'll all freeze to death. Operation L.E.A.F must happen and we need to start planning today," said Ray.

"Consider me in. What do I need to do?" asked Flounder.

"I need you to manage. How good are you at managing?" asked Ray.

"I manage to brush my teeth every morning. I'm very self-conscience about my teeth. I really don't want mandibular teeth problems," said Flounder.

"Great. I'll need to count on you to manage the day-to-day operations of this plan," said Ray.

"I'm there for you. Always will be," said Flounder.

****

"Brunch time. Brunch time," yelled the Guards, opening the cell doors. "Please line up and proceed to the cafeteria overlooking the sundeck."

"Sundeck? Why aren't we going to the main hall overlooking the pavilion?" asked Pom.

"Something about they're remodeling again," said Gil.

"This place is such a hell hole," said Pom.

"Morning Pom, Gil, how are you?" asked Ray who happened to line up behind them.

"Morning Ray. How did you sleep last night?" asked Pom.

"Not bad. I was a little sweaty. The new down comforters they issued us are almost too warm."

"I agree," said Pom.

"You guys sitting next to anyone at brunch?" asked Ray.

"Just the usual," said Pom.

"Mind if Flounder and I join you?" asked Ray.

"No problem. I think it'll be good to sit with different people. I know The Queen Mary encourages us to make acquaintances. Probably be a good way to strengthen our acquaintanceship," said Pom.

Pom, Gil, Ray, and Flounder all lined up in serving area four and picked up their silverware, coffee cups, plates, and napkins. "Proceed to the omelet station," the guard yelled out.

"What if I don't want anything in my omelet?" whispered Flounder to Ray.

"I don't know. This is my first time. Just shake your head and maybe they'll let you have it plain," Ray whispered back.

"Next," the guard yelled to Flounder.

"Toppings?" asked the guard.

"None," replied Flounder.

"Toppings," stated the guard.

"None," said Flounder.

"Toppings," yelled the guard.

"Egg wash?" said Flounder. "Very well," the guard removed a small brush and dipped it in a nearby bowl of peacock egg and wiped the top of the omelet with extra egg.

"Next," yelled the guard.

"Toppings?" asked the guard to Ray.

"Do you have any veal?" Ray asked.

"Yes," replied the guard and filled the omelet with fresh veal. "Next."

Pom and Gil joined Ray and Flounder already sitting at a table located near the back of the room. "These eggs taste funny. Too fresh or something," said Gil.

"Listen. I have to ask something. I've been thinking lately. This place is not the place for me," said Ray. "The food is terrible. The sleep conditions are unbearable. I probably only take part in 30 percent of the daily activities they provide us. I really feel that The

Queen Mary does not have our best interests in mind. I've been thinking of making a change," said Ray.

"Change? Like what?" asked Pom.

"I'm looking to change my situation here in the dungeon and leaving this place. Leaving this town," said Ray.

"What? How? Wait, what?" asked Pom in disbelief.

"Why would you leave?" asked Gil.

"Why would I leave? Why would I leave? Look around you. You are surrounded by dungeon walls. Even worse, if and when you are set free from this Almighty awful place, you are still surrounded by walls. City walls," yelled Ray.

"Well, the city walls keep us safe from intruders and mold," said Gil.

"Intruders ," scoffed Ray. "Like the time the wall kept out that band of non-believers and they just used step ladders to jump over the wall. Remember how they beat a bunch of us up and giggled as they ran through the city gate?" said Ray. "And as far as mold is concerned, there's more mold in that blue cheese dressing you have on our omelet than there is mold on the outside of those walls," said Ray.

"But the mold in my dressing is green. Not black," said Gil.

"Black mold, green mold, whatever. Listen. I don't give a shit about mold. Or intruders. I just want my tap shoes back and I want to be able to please people with the sweet, sweet sound of my tappers clacking. Is that so much to ask? If I can't do it here. I'm going to leave this town and do it somewhere else. Flounder is with me. What do you guys say? Can I count on you? Do you want to leave or what?" ask Ray holding out his index finger for approval.

"I'm in," said Pom.

"I'm in too, but I don't think it's a good idea," said Gil.

"Great. Then let's touch tips and Flounder will manage your availability for planning." The four simultaneously touched index fingers signifying trust in Blueburrie and quietly finished their omelets.

"Line up. There's doggy bags if you need them. Not that you have any pets in your cells," yelled the guard.

"Yeah. Most of your pets probably have starved by now," laughed the guard. Ray and Flounder lined up behind Hu and Apricot.

"Hi Hu," said Ray.

"Hi. Have you met Ape?" asked Hu.

"There's an ape in this dungeon?" asked Ray.

"Yeah, she's standing right in front you. Her name is Apricot."

"But people call me Ape," interrupted Ape.

"Oh, nice to meet you," whispered Ray.

"Listen. I really need to talk to you Hu. Is there a chance we can talk at lunch in a couple hours?" asked Ray.

"Why not talk now?" asked Ape.

"Because, Ape, we're in line and we're not supposed to be talking," whispered Flounder.

"No. I mean, we can talk through the cracks in our cells," said Ape.

"We can do that? How?" said Ray.

"Well, I've lived in these dungeons for a very long time. Each crack in our cells is connected to other cells. If you whisper in your crack," said Ape.

"And you figure out what crack is connected where," interrupted Ray. "We can talk to each other without the guards knowing. Ape, you're a genius."

"Thanks, Ray," Ape smiled and moved a little closer to Hu, grabbing his hand.

Hu looked at her, and thought it was odd she grabbed his hand. Does Ape Like me? he thought. "Only time can tell," Hu accidently said out loud.

"Only time can tell if she's a genius?" asked Ray.

"Yeah. That's what I meant," said Hu while blushing.

The prisoners were led back to their cells and the doors slammed shut. "Lunch will be served in a few hours," yelled one of the guards. "I hope you saved room for non-shucked oysters," the guards said laughing down the hallway.

"I wonder if it's true what Ape said about the cracks," said Flounder.

"Only one way to find out," said Ray. Moving his hands along the wall above Mrs. Warwick's bunk Ray found a large horizonal crack in the wall. "Hello?" he whispered into the crack. He carefully listened to the wall to see if he could hear a response.

"Try again," said Flounder. "Hello?" said Ray.

"Who's this?" a mysterious response came from the what seemed to be within the wall.

"It's me, Ray McJohnson" whispered Ray.

"Hi Ray. Guess who this is?" said the mysterious voice. Ray looked at Flounder whose mouth was open in astonishment.

"It really works. Who do you think it is? Oh Almighty, it could be The Queen Mary herself," said Flounder.

Ray looked at Flounder in a slight panic and said, "The Queen Mary?" with a big gulp.

"No. Silly. It's me, Ape,"

"Ape, is that you? What are the odds, I'd pick your crack?" said Ray.

"Pretty small," said Ape.

"There has to be a hundred cracks in this cell," said Ray.

"And each crack is linked to another prisoner. Try another one," said Ape.

"Flounder, come here and manage this crack," said Ray as he went to the other side of the cell to find another crack. Flounder went over to the crack above Mrs. Warwick's bunk and wrote 'Ape's Crack'.

"Hello. Who's there?" said Ray, whispering into a slightly smaller vertical crack this time.

"Is someone talking to me?" said the response from the crack.

125

"Yes. It's me. Ray,"

"Ray? Is that you?" said the mysterious voice.

"Yes. It's me. Who is this? Who's speaking?" asked Ray.

"It's Mosh."

"Mosh? What are you doing here?" asked Ray.

"Isn't it obvious? I'm talking to you through this crack," Mosh said and snickered.

"No, I mean what are you doing in this dungeon?" asked Ray.

"Well, The Queen Mary put me here. She wanted me to pluck some fucking eyelashes from some peacock and I didn't do it. To be honest, I'm not a hundred-percent sure how I would even accomplish that task," said Mosh.

"I guess I would have just grabbed any peacock by the neck off the street and pulled out it's eyelashes," said Ray.

"Yeah, no shit. Well, what do you want?" asked Mosh.

"We're looking to break out of this dungeon. We're tired of The Queen Mary setting all sorts of new rules, and we truly believe that there's a better life outside of Blueburrie. Plus, she took away my tappers and I desperately need to get them back," said Ray.

"I'm in," said Mosh.

"What?"

"I'm in," said Mosh. "This place sucks and quite honestly, so does The Queen Mary. I need a fresh start and getting out of Blueburrie is my best bet," said Mosh.

"Great. Flounder will manage your role and we'll get you details soon," said Ray.

Ray ran over to the crack labelled "Ape" and began to whisper. "It worked. I was able to contact other people through different cracks," he said.

"I told you. There isn't a person in this whole dungeon you can't talk to," Ape said.

"Is Hu there?" asked Ray.

"He sure is, just a minute," said Ape.

"This is Hu," he whispered.

"Hu. This is Ray. Listen. I didn't get to talk to you earlier in the cafeteria. I'm looking to form an operation to get the hell out of this dreadful place. We even plan to leave the city all together and start a new life somewhere else," said Ray.

Hu thought for a moment. Leaving this dungeon was one thing, but leaving his uncle? It was always a dream of his to start his own butcher shop. "Do you think wherever you're going will have a butcher shop?" asked Hu.

"Probably not. If you're looking to start your own, I don't think there'd be a better time," Ray said.

"I'm a real believer in signs," said Hu. "I really think that we were placed in this dungeon together for a reason. I don't think it's happenstance that our cracks are connected and we're whispering in them. Ray, I'm in. I'll join the operation," said Hu.

"Great. I'll have Flounder send you the welcome packet with some details on Operation L.E.A.F. Welcome to the start of your new life," said Ray.

****

"What did Ray want?" asked Ape.

"Oh. Nothing much," said Hu.

"Didn't sound like nothing much," said Ape.

"He was just saying that they plan to escape this dungeon and leave the city somehow and start a new life. I thought it through for a second and decided to join them," said Hu.

"You did? Doesn't it sound dangerous?" Ape asked.

"It does, but I've worked my whole life for my uncle. It was always my dream to meet a nice girl, settle down, and open my own butcher shop someday. I know everything there is to know about meat and I really think now's my big chance," said Hu.

"Your meat sounds delicious to me," Ape said as she sat down right next to Hu on the bunk.

"My meat is delicious. Juicy. Salty. Just the perfect amount of grease," said Hu.

"I love grease," Ape said as she moved even closer.

"My peacocks are always roasted just perfect," said Hu.

"What about your legs. Do you have nice legs?" asked Ape.

"My legs? They're great. The meat falls right off the bone."

"And your breasts?" asked Ape.

"My breasts? They're huge. Biggest peacock breasts in town," said Hu. The two inmates locked eyes and an awkward moment fell between them. The moonlight shone through the cell window on to Ape's face. Hu thought to himself just how beautiful Ape looked at that moment, but his insecurities lead him to believe that she couldn't possibly be in love with him. He looked away and nervously said, "I guess a big part of my plan is to settle down with someone. I'm great at being a butcher, but I need a wife to help clean the butcher shop."

"I know how to sweep. I'm not bad at scrubbing either. I even have a bucket and a mop," Ape said.

"You do? You might be the perfect fit for my butcher shop," he said with a smile.

"I'd clean your shop any time," said Ape. The two laughed and embraced.

"You're a great acquaintance, Ape," said Hu.

"I like you too," said Ape.

****

"So, Ray, Flounder, Hu, Ape, Pom, Gil, and Mosh. That's the team so far," said Flounder.

"Don't forget about me," said Mrs. Warwick.

"That's right, Mrs. Warwick. We'll need to get those books of knowledge Professor Warwick wrote. Once we break out of this dungeon, those books are going to be essential if we're going to survive outside the walls of Blueburrie," said Ray.

"I'm pretty sure I know exactly where they are. Almost positive. Like eighty-five percent. No lower than seventy-five percent sure. If I had to bet, I'd say there's a fifty-fifty chance I'll remember," said Mrs. Warwick.

"I like those odds," said Flounder.

"Yeah, I guess those are good numbers. I never learned percentages in school, so I'll just put my faith in you," said Ray.

"What about a ship? We're going to need some sort of ship to aid in our escape," said Ray.

"Do you think that Captain Limb might be interested? I heard his whole crew is currently serving some time and they're in the dungeon as we speak," said Flounder.

"This surely can't be a coincidence. I wonder if they would be interested in leaving this place?" asked Ray.

"If they're as unhappy as us, I'd say there's a fifty-fifty chance they'd join us," said Flounder.

"I think I like those odds," said Ray. "Let's find Captain Limb's crack and see if he'll respond."

Ray and Flounder fanned out and started searching for cracks located in the walls of their cell. A series of large vertical cracks were visible through the outer wall.

"These cracks are pretty small," said Flounder.

"You know I had an uncle in the dungeon wall repair business. He always said that the bad thing about cracks is that they are larger on the outside. So, if the cracks are small on the inside of the wall, imagine what they look like on the outside?" said Ray.

"Good to know," said Flounder.

"Let's start whispering. Remember, we're only looking for Captain Limb. If anyone else answers, button your lips and hush," said Ray.

"Ray, Ray, I think I found Captain Limb. I keep talking to someone that keeps referring to himself using the pronoun me. Don't all the deckhands on The Queen Mary, the Cog refer to themselves that way?" asked Flounder.

"They sure do. Step aside. Let me talk to him. Who is this?" asked Ray.

"Who I?" said the voice through the crack.

"Hello Who-i. My name is Ray McJohnson, and I currently live in cell 21. I'm here with my acquaintance, Flounder. Is Captain Limb available by any chance?"

"He's napping. Can me take a message?" said the deckhand. Ray hesitated for a second considering the risky nature of the topic, but decided to leave a message anyway.

"Yes. This is Ray. I'm planning an escape and I was wondering if he would be interested in joining our plan. We would need to use his Cog, and we'd like to sail away to a new land and start a new life," said Ray.

"Hold on. You're going too fast. So this is Ray," said the deckhand.

"Yes. Ray. Like I was saying we're planning an escape."

"Okay, planning an escape and what else?" interrupted the deckhand.

"We want to know if Captain Limb would be interested in joining our operation and."

"Interested in joining our operation," interrupted the deckhand.

"Right. Join our operation and we were wondering if we could use his Cog and find a new life in a new city."

"Use his Cog, and what else?" said the deckhand.

"Use his Cog and travel to a new land and find a new life," said Ray.

"Find a new life where?" said the deckhand.

"New City. Not Blueburrie," said Ray.

"New life in a new city. Got it," said the deckhand.

"Oh Great," said Ray.

"Me'll be sure he gets the message. Oh wait. He's up. Did you want to talk to him now?" asked the deckhand.

"Yes. Please," said Ray.

"This is Captain Limb. How can I help you?"

"Captain Limb. My name is Ray McJohnson. I was wondering if I could have a moment of your time. I'll keep my story brief. You see, I'm a tapper in The Queen Mary's entertain division. I was born in a small cottage in the north end of Blueburrie. By the age of three years old, my parents knew I had a special skill. Before I could even walk, I would paradiddle around the house. My mother always said I was something special, and by my fourth birthday my parents encouraged me to strap wooden planks to my feet so I could make that sweet sound of tap. I've lived in Blueburrie my whole life. Most of my years, I've never really had any interest in exploring out of my comfort zone or the city of Blueburrie. I met my best acquaintance, Flounder when I was very young and we have been best acquaintances our whole life. He's always by my side and he will do anything for me. When he and I were teenagers, we took a job cutting royal bushes alongside the castle. It was a good job, but I always felt I wanted more. It was Flounder who gave me the courage I needed to try out for The Queen Mary's entertainment division as a tap dancer. He always told me that I had the skills, so why shouldn't I at least try. I slept in and didn't make the first round of tryouts, which really discouraged me. The next round of tryouts I still didn't quality. That only gave me more motivation to try harder. The third and fourth round of tryouts, I missed because I had peacock shit in my tappers. By the fifth round of tryouts, I was ready to show my stuff. My buffalo was strong, and Cincinnati was at the top of its game. I dig toed into a cramp roll without breaking a sweat and I could spank, slap, and slide all day long. Unfortunately, I had a bad case of whale hives and vomited on the stage before I could perform. I went into a severe depression and skipped the seventh, eighth, and ninth tryouts. By the grace of the almighty, Flounder got me rolling again, and by the tenth tryout, I performed perfect. The Queen Mary approved my membership into the entertainment group as an intern and Flounder and I were the happiest simpletons in the whole town of Blueburrie. Years passed and I was happy as can be. I loved performing at balls, gathering, parties, and galas. You may have seen me perform before?" asked Ray.

"Huh?" said Captain Limb.

"Perform. At balls and galas? Never mind it's not that important. What's important is that at the last friendship ball, The Queen Mary decided that my paradiddle. My paradiddle of all things was off center. I think she was crazy," said Ray.

"I think so too," said Flounder.

"At any rate, she went bat shit crazy and started screaming. She ended up throwing my only pair of tappers into the community pond and sentenced me to 182 months in the dungeon. The reason for the whisper chat today is we're looking to break out of this hell hole. We need your crew and your Cog to escape to a new life. What do you think? You willing to dedicate your life and crew's life to help us and join us?" asked Ray.

"What? I'm sorry, the last thing I heard was I'll be brief. We must be using a damp crack," said Captain Limb.

"But listen, I'm not sure if you're interested, but we're looking to break out of this dungeon. My deckhands have already informed me that most of them fit through the bars on the windows and for those of us that don't we could probably squeeze out using some melted butter, if we had any," said Captain Limb. Ray and Flounder looked at each other.

"Say yes," whispered Flounder.

Ray leaned into the crack and whispered, "Yes."

"Great," said Captain Limb. "I'll chat with you again soon and we can work out a plan. I look forward to working with you." Ray and Flounder embraced and began to laugh and smile. "Things are happening now for sure," they said as they ran over to Mrs. Warwick and all embraced again in joy. "We're going to get out of here," they all said while cheering.

Chapter Fourteen

THE DOOR LABELLED BACK

D own at the buttery, Chef Will and First Lieutenant were busy cooking up a batch of unsalted butter. Drops of sweat dripped off of Chef Will's forehead while stirring the butter in vat 10.

"How much longer do we have to stay here?" asked Chef Will. "I feel like we've been here for several weeks."

"It has been several weeks. If we try and sneak out, we'll blow our cover," said First Lieutenant.

"I swear I think we've buttered nearly 300 sticks by now, and since we're interns, we haven't seen a single pacecado," said Chef Will.

"I know. I know. But we have to play the part. If we get caught now, all this butter and hard work we've done will be for nothing. If there was some way to get in touch with the captain. I must know he's okay."

"How you boys doing this morning. Almighty damn, if that isn't a great color on that butter. As yellow as my eyes. How's it taste? Salty?" ask Kent.

"Shouldn't be. This is an unsalted batch," said Chef Will while slapping a fresh slab of butter on to a nearby table for sticking.

"That slab ready to be sticked?" Kent asked.

"Yes, sir," said First Lieutenant.

"Well. Let me help. You know, back in my day I could stick up to 30 sticks an hour. They called me slappy hands and I won several awards for sticking," said Kent.

"I think my daughter would be proud of me if she knew just how much butter I could stick in an hour."

133

"You really miss her?" said First Lieutenant.

"Miss her? I hardly know her. I miss her every day. She's stuck in that almighty damned castle. I know she's got a good job. She works for The Queen Mary herself, but I sometimes get that sense, call it a third sense, a parent's intuition, she just isn't happy," said Kent.

"You mean a sense like sight or smell?" asked Chef Will. "Yeah, similar, but not. If only there was some way to get in touch with her," said Kent.

"You know, we really have something in common," said First Lieutenant. "Remember last week when you had us fill out those on-boarding papers and one of the forms asked if we currently were hiding from The Queen Mary's guards. We answered, no. Although, that really wasn't the case," said First Lieutenant.

"What?" said Kent. "Well. We're not entirely sure if the guards are looking for us, per say. In reality, we're deck mates on The Queen Mary, the Cog. A few weeks ago, The Queen Mary incarcerated all the deckhands and the Captain himself," said First Lieutenant.

"Captain Limb?" asked Kent.

"The very same. He was taken to the dungeon, we haven't seen him since," said First Lieutenant. "Captain Limb and I were good acquaintances back in higher learning school. Our first job was trimming bushes near the castle. He decided to follow his father in sailing and I took a liking to butter and creaming things. I haven't seen him for years. You say he's being held at the dungeon?" asked Kent.

"Yes. He's there with the whole crew of deckhands of The Queen Mary, the Cog. Chef Will and I need to contact him and try to get them out. As long as we're heading there, this might be a good time to see your daughter Margarine," said First Lieutenant.

"You make some valid points. Let me check my schedule. I think I might be able to move some meetings around and come with," said Kent.

****

"Twinkle, twinkle little stump. How I wonder why you grump," Margarine sang, getting The Queen Mary's schmock prepared for the day ahead. "Good morning Hornco, how did you sleep?" Hornco just shrugged and scattered over to the nearby window. "I slept pretty well myself. Only two night terrors last night. Anything below three and I'm pretty well rested in the morning. So overall it was a good night," said Margarine. Hornco looked out the window at the peacocks basking in the sun below. In the distance a small speck in the sky seemed to be getting closer and closer to the window. Hornco kept his eyes focused, as the spot got bigger and bigger. Blue in color, Hornco now realized it was a blue jay flying straight for the window.

"What are you pointing at?" asked Margarine. Hornco continued to point at the blue jay getting closer and closer. "What is it? Is it your foot? Did you hurt it?" she asked. Hornco just kept pointing. "What's wrong? Is this some type of new dance you wanted to show me? Are you stretching? What are you trying to say? Should I leave?" Margarine began to yell in confusion. Hornco just kept feverishly pointing at the window. "Maybe you're trying to tell me something about the window. Should I look?" asked Margarine. "I really wish you would use your words, Hornco. I can't read your mind," Margarine said now getting annoyed by the whole situation. "Fine. I'll look."

Just as Margarine looked out the window, she realized that it was a blue jay flying straight for the window. At the very last second she opened the window and the blue jay flew in and landed on the bedpost nearby. "A blue jay? For me? I've never received one before," Margarine grabbed the blue jay by the neck and tore the message off attached to his leg. The bird squawked in pain for a second.

"You'll be fine," said Margarine opening the little note. *Margarine. It's your father, Kent. I'm coming to talk to you. Be prepared.*

I will meet you at the back door of the castle in two days. Count to 400,005 immediately after the sun sets and I will be there. Don't forget to finish your butter. Love Kent. "This is wonderful. Hornco, my father! You can finally meet my father. Come to think of it, it's been so long, I feel like I'll be meeting him too," Margarine jumped around and danced in joy. She was so excited to see her father again. "Oh Hornco. I can hardly wait. I'm so very excited." Hornco shrugged. "Oh Hornco. Get excited. This is very exciting. This is a huge deal. You're going to love my father and I guarantee he's going to love you too."

****

"I sent the jay to my daughter. If there's a way we can get to talk to Captain Limb, I think she's the key to getting inside," said Kent.

"If it's anything like the complicated handle you have on the door to your buttery, we'll never get in," scoffed First Lieutenant.

"Don't be salty. You were turning the handle the wrong way," said Chef Will.

"No I wasn't," said First Lieutenant.

"Yes, you were," said Chef Will.

"Enough. It doesn't matter. I finally get to see my daughter and I'm excited with joy to be able to see her again," said Kent.

"Likewise, it's been too long that I haven't seen Captain Limb. We need to get him out of that hell hole. When do we plan to leave?" asked First Lieutenant.

"In two days. I let Margarine know that we will see her at precisely 400,005 counts after sunset at the back door of the castle," said Kent.

"What should we do until then?" asked Chef Will.

"Anyone up for making some butter?" said Kent.

"Sure," replied Chef Will and First Lieutenant.

****

The sun was just about to set on the town of Blueburrie. Peacocks were gathering sticks to make nests to bed down for the night. Throughout the city there was the scent of peacock roasting and stewed. Families began to say their dinner prayers, thanking The Queen Mary for their wonderful lives. In the dark alley beside Fourth Avenue, First Lieutenant, Chef Will, and Kent scampered down the road hiding behind garbage cans to conceal their identity. "We have to run fast and get to the back door without anyone seeing us," whispered Kent. The three kept running when Kent held up his fist and whispered,

"Hide."

Chef Will and First Lieutenant slid behind a garbage can and ducked down for cover.

"Look," whispered Chef Will. "Someone threw out a perfectly good blue fin tuna sandwich. What kind of animal doesn't finish their blue fin?" asked Chef Will.

"No kidding. I'll take a bite," said First Lieutenant.

"Does it taste a little off?" asked Chef Will.

"Maybe a little," said First Lieutenant.

"What are you two doing?" asked Kent.

"We found this blue fin tuna sandwich practically laying on top of the garbage in this can. Want a bite?" said Chef Will.

"We don't have time for this. We have to meet my daughter. How do I look?" said Kent.

"You look great. Your shoes are really shiny," said First Lieutenant.

"You think so? I really need to install a full-length mirror in the bathroom at the buttery. It was hard applying a fresh coat of butter polish to them without it," said Kent. "Now finish your sandwich and let's go."

Margarine snuck past the guards and ran down the long hallway in the castle. Hornco jogged next to her, trying to keep up.

"Keep up," said Margarine. She ran past the kitchen, and ballroom C. She ran up two flights of stairs into another hallway with blowing tapestries in the windows. Back down another set of stairs, she jumped off the last two stairs in excitement. "Keep up," she yelled at Hornco again. He was having trouble getting down the stairs. "If you can't keep up jump on my shoulder. We still have quite a long way to go," Margarine yelled while grabbing Hornco off the ground. Margarine's jog started picking up speed until she was in a full sprint. She ran back down the long hallway labeled "Long Hallway" and through a set of double doors. Back up a set of stairs and then immediately taking the corner she went back down a set of stairs. Who designed this castle? Am I lost? she thought for a second while still running as fast as she could.

"There's the door," she said noticing a sign on a door labeled "back." She pushed the door open with a magical force and there stood her father; Kent, First Lieutenant, and Chef Will.

"Margarine?" said Kent.

"Kent?" said Margarine.

"Is that you?" the two said in harmony. They immediately hugged and embraced.

"Kent, you smell just like I always imagined. Like warm butter," said Margarine.

"Call me Dad," said Kent while holding back his tears. "I can't believe it's you. I just can't believe it. Do I have any brothers or sisters?" asked Margarine.

"No," said Kent.

"I'm an only child? Just like Hornco. Dad. I want you to meet someone. This is my best acquaintance Hornco," Margarine said.

Kent looked around for a second not noticing anyone in sight. "You must have your mother's legs. Clearly, you've outrun your acquaintance, Hornco," Kent said.

"No silly. Hornco is a vole. He's right here," Hornco pointed at Kent while he perched on Margarine's shoulder.

"Nice to meet you, vole. I mean, Hornco," said Kent.

"I really hate to break up the family love festival, but we don't have much time. I need to talk to Captain Limb. Would you be able to get him a message?" said First Lieutenant. "I'm not very good with messages. I always forget them unless they rhyme," said Margarine.

"Rhyme?" asked First Lieutenant.

"Yes. You know. Like Mary had a humongous mole, it's hair as black coal," said Margarine. First Lieutenant and Chef Will looked at each other and shrugged.

"You have any bright ideas?" asked Chef Will.

"I guess, I'll do my best," said First Lieutenant. "Oh Captain Limb, oh Captain Limb, I had to go for a swim. For you see." First Lieutenant paused to think of the next word.

"You're doing great," said Chef Will.

"For you see, it's me, First Lieutenant, who feels so abstinent. Oh forget it. This plan will never work," First Lieutenant said, kicking a nearby rock with his foot.

"I'm sorry. I just can't remember things unless they are in rhyme," said Margarine.

"Did you want me to go and just get Captain Limb, so you can talk to him yourself?" asked Margarine.

"You can do that? Well, that eliminates the whole need for a messenger," said First Lieutenant.

"Sure, it's no problem. I'll be right back," said Margarine closing the back door of the castle.

"I can't believe she can just go get any prisoner she wants," said Chef Will.

"Can you believe how beautiful she is? She looks just like her mother. At least I think she does. It was a long time ago. I met her mother in a town called Snurburrie. We were so young. I was pre-ballin' pretty heavy that night when I met this beautiful woman. Her hair greasy, like butter. Her face, shiney. Her thighs. Oh how her thighs melted me like butter. We met on the dance floor. We instantly connected. Our passion was uncontrollable. We ran off and made sweet love behind a pillory. Thank the almighty that the prisoner was sleeping at the time or that would have been quite embarrassing. We made love for a few minutes and parted ways. I never saw her again, until one day when she sent me a jay saying I was going to be a father. I simply responded. 'Great. Let's name her Margarine'," said Kent.

"That's a beautiful story. I still can't believe they just let Margarine take any prisoner she wants out of their cell?" said Chef Will.

"No kidding," said First Lieutenant.

The door labeled "back" sprang open and there stood Captain Limb and Margarine.

"First Lieutenant?"

"Captain Limb, is that you?" said First Lieutenant. They immediately embraced. "Captain Limb, you smell just like I imagined. Like warm shit," said First Lieutenant.

"I probably don't smell great. There is severe overcrowding in my cell. We're only supposed to have around four and a half prisoners in each, and we have nearly five times that," said Captain Limb.

"Are they treating you well?" asked First Lieutenant.

"I mean the food isn't bad. No worse than Chef Will's, no offense," Captain Limb said while giving Chef Will a stern glance. "We get massages every day. The steam room sometimes is a little warm, but hardly anything to complain about," said Captain Limb.

"Listen, we're going to get you out of here. The whole crew too," said First Lieutenant.

"The whole crew?" asked Captain Limb.

"Yeah, the whole crew," said First Lieutenant.

"Did you want me to go and get them?" Margarine said while eavesdropping on the conversation.

"No, not today. We need to think of a master plan. A great escape plan," said First Lieutenant.

"I met this prisoner the other day while talking into his crack. He said he's got a group of people looking to escape. Ray McSomething," said Captain Limb.

"His crack?" asked First Lieutenant.

"Yeah, that's pretty much how we communicate in here. We talk into each other's cracks," said Captain Limb.

"I'll try and schedule a meeting with him and I'll let you know the details," said Captain Limb.

"Great. I look forward to you breaking out of this place," said First Lieutenant.

"I agree. I can't wait either. I should probably be getting back to my cell," said Captain Limb.

"We'll be in touch," said First Lieutenant "It was so nice seeing you, Kent. I mean, Dad," said Margarine.

"It was truly a blessing seeing you too. Margarine. I wanted to ask you. Are you truly happy? Is The Queen Mary treating you well?" asked Kent.

"Happy? I don't know. Define happy. I mean, The Queen Mary yells a lot. She calls me stupid and a simpleton, but I don't blame her for that. I make a lot of mistakes. I probably deserve the verbal lashings," said Margarine.

"I've talked quite a bit with Hornco about sometimes leaving this place. I know that The Queen Mary would never allow it. She can't really get dressed in the morning without my help, so my gut tells me she would never let me leave. But I have thought about it. I really have," said Margarine.

"Think about it more. I hate to see you unhappy. It pains me to know that I live an amazing life at the buttery and you are trapped in this castle. I overheard First Lieutenant talking to Captain Limb. I believe they are planning an escape,"

"An escape?" asked Margarine.

"An escape to a better life," said Kent. "I want you to consider it."

"Could Hornco come too?" asked Margarine.

"I'm sure we could make some room for a small vole such as Hornco," said Kent.

"I'll send you a jay in a few days time. I want you to think about leaving and reply then," The two embraced once more and Margarine closed the door labeled back as First Lieutenant, Chef Will, and Kent headed for the alley to hurry back to the buttery.

Chapter Fifteen

PLAN SEA

❧

Deep in the dungeon, the prisoners were wrapping up their yoga session. "Move forward, line up, and proceed to your cells," yelled the guards.

"Listen on the main crack tonight," one deckhand whispered to another. "There's going to be a meeting tonight. Ray and Flounder wanted us to pass the word on." The deckhand nodded, and began to whisper down the line to get the word out.

"Close all cells. Candles out. See you tomorrow prisoners," the guards said laughing down the hall.

"We surely will see them tomorrow. That's for sure," another guard laughed.

"This crack system is pretty amazing. Who knew we could communicate with each other through the cracks, or we could all talk together using this massive crack in the ceiling," Ray said while standing on a chair near the ceiling crack.

"It is very convenient," replied Hu.

"It's really a great way to plan an escape," said Pom.

"Seems pretty convenient, I just wish I could see the other person who is talking," said Gil.

"I just wish I had a fucking chair to stand on. It's hard to hear you guys sometimes," said Mosh.

"Isn't there a chair next to your writing desk?" asked Ray.

"No," said Mosh.

"I'd lend you a dining room chair, but the guards took most of mine away," said Porksmu who was now part of Operation L.E.A.F..

"Well, that does me no good now, does it?" Mosh yelled.

"I used to have a set of four chairs. The guards took all of them and left me with one. I'll never get to a host a dinner party with just one chair," said Porksmu.

"Who the fuck cares about dinner parties? When was the last time you were able to host any type of parties in your cell?" asked Mosh.

"I'm not saying I want to host a party any time soon. I'm saying I wish I had the option to someday host a party," said Porksmu.

"I think we're getting a little off topic," whispered Flounder.

"Flounder's right. If we manage to escape this dungeon, Porksmu, you'll be able to have all the dinner parties you can manage. Now, I want to start with Plan A: brute force. We overtake the guards during our steam room time. Since they always leave the doors unlocked, we could subdue them, run out the door labelled "side," and head for the harbor. Gil did provide some constructive criticism on that plan considering that during steam time most of us are naked. So, if we do manage to make it out on the street we're going to be running around naked and pretty easy to spot," said Ray.

"I don't want to be running around with my pecker hanging out," said Hu.

"I wouldn't mind that," said Ape while giving Hu a smile.

"Plan A certainly has some risks and nudity is one of them," said Ray.

"Plan B is a two-part operation with 16 sub sections. This plan is going to depend on how many extra sets of cell door keys we can obtain. Porksmu, you're confident that you can duplicate the cell door keys if we save our clam shells from oyster night, correct?" asked Ray.

"Well, clam shells and oyster shells are two different things. I don't think we can make clam shells out of oyster shells," said Gil.

"My mistake Gil. I meant oyster shells. If we saved our oyster shells from oyster night," said Ray.

"If you can get me the shells, I can reproduce the keys. Already have most of the tools to do it," said Porksmu.

"When you say most of the tools, what other tools do you need?" asked Ray.

"Well, I've got my safety goggles, safety gloves and hammer. Just need a key duplicator chisel and I'm all set," said Porksmu.

"Does anyone know where we can find a key duplicator chisel?" asked Ray.

"Me think that me saw one the other day in the kitchen, but me not entirely sure," said a random deckhand.

"Well, that's another problem to this plan. We'll need to get our hands on that key duplicator. If we manage to get the key duplicator, then Porksmu can make us all cell door keys. On the night of the full moon, the plan would be to knock sixteen times on your cell door. On the sixteenth knock, we all turn our keys clockwise opening our cells at precisely the same moment. Once our cell doors are open, we'll take off our shoes and toss them out the window to Margarine below." asked Ray. Silence was the only response from the crack, while Ray listened for any sign of Margarine.

"Well. I'll assume that."

"I'm here. I'm here," said Margarine. "My crack is pretty small. You probably couldn't hear me. I'm in. Hornco and I are ready to tackle anything you can throw at us," said Margarine.

"Great," said Ray. "Well expect to have about eighty pairs of shoes thrown at you on that night. After we have our shoes off, we'll sneak down the main corridor," said Ray.

"What happens if we see any guards?" asked Pom.

"Well, that's part 2: sub section seven. We're going to split up into two teams. Team one will be the decoys and team two will be the bait. If we see any guards team one will run like hell as the decoys and team two will also run like hell as bait. Either way, both teams will need to run as fast as they can," said Ray.

"Once we're by the door labelled front, the final step of the plan is to line up. Flounder, you'll be in the front. You'll need to press your body flush against the door and everyone will line up behind Flounder. Leave no space in between you and the person in front of you. Once we have all lined up. Mrs. Warwick, you'll run as fast as you can and push the massive line of prisoners. Hopefully the chain reaction and pressure will build up so high that it'll force the door labelled front right open, giving us access to freedom. Margarine, hopefully, by then you'll have time to organize all of our shoes and we can run for the harbor where First Lieutenant should be waiting for us with The Queen Mary, the Cog prepped and ready to sail.

"I don't think this plan will work," said Gil.

"What don't you like about it?" asked Ray.

"All of it," said Gil. "Well. So far we have plan A and plan B. Do you have any ideas?" asked Ray.

"No," said Gil.

"Well, it's all we got so far," said Ray.

"Well there is plan sea," said Flounder.

"Plan sea. I know. It's risky and certainly has a lot of dependencies, especially on butter," said Ray.

"I think it's worth discussing. Depending on each other is how we get through things," said Flounder.

"You're right, Flounder. I'll let you talk about plan sea," said Ray.

"My vote would be plan sea," said Captain Limb.

"You haven't heard any of the details yet," yelled Mosh.

"Well, anything to do with the sea, is for me," said Captain Limb.

Flounder adjusted his half shirt and pulled up his pants revealing his ankles. "Plan Sea. Hopefully you're all sitting down and ready to hear the plan of a lifetime," said Flounder. "This plan is huge. It's the biggest plan I've ever dreamed up. It's going to require each of us to participate. We'll need everyone to do their part or it won't work. It all starts with Mrs. Warwick and Margarine. The night before the big escape we'll need Margarine to let Mrs. Warwick out the door labelled back. At this point, Mrs. Warwick will run to her house and get Professor Warwick's journals. It's very important you get all the journals and don't leave any information behind. Once you have the journals return to the castle and Margarine will let you back in," said Flounder.

"No problem, I think I know exactly where the journals are," said Mrs. Warwick.

"On the same night, we'll need Captain Limb to send a jay to First Lieutenant and Chef Will letting them know to bring a couple sticks of butter to the prison the night of the escape. The plan is to use the butter to grease up the bars on the windows of the dungeon. If we grease up the bars, we should be able to all squeeze through no problem. Ray, I'll need you to send a jay to your cousin, Toss. Let him know we're all coming and to be ready for us in Snurburrie. Hu and Ape. On the night before the escape, Margarine can let you out the door labelled back and I'll need you to gather as much peacock jerky, peacock steaks, cheeks, ankles, and beaks as you can and carry it to The Queen Mary, the Cog. We'll need lots of food if we're going to make the journey to Snurburrie," said Flounder.

"Do you want any peacock thighs?" asked Hu.

"Yuck. Leave those behind," said Flounder. "Once you have loaded up the boat, come right back and Margarine will let you in."

"What the fuck should I do?" interrupted Mosh. "I was just getting to your part," said Flounder. "I think we'll really want to have a celebration ball once we arrive safely at our new town of Snurburrie. So as acting ball manager, please start planning for a grand ball to take place once we arrive. Pom and Gil, I'll need you two retrieve Ray's tapper shoes. During judgement day, The Queen Mary ordered they be ripped off Ray's feet and thrown into the community pond. I think the tap shoes are still at the bottom of that pond. I'll need you guys to retrieve them and meet us at the Harbor," said Flounder.

"Should be easy," said Pom.

"Probably will only take an hour," said Gil.

"Great. Dr Dunston and Deckhands, when Chef Will and First Lieutenant arrive with the butter the night of the escape, I'll need you grease up the bars of the windows so everyone can squeeze out. Don't be shy with the butter. We should have plenty to get those bars greased up.

Margarine, have you seen Hornco?" asked Flounder.

"I saw him earlier. I think he's out for his late night jog around the dungeon," she said. At that moment a small shadow appeared under the crack of Ray and Flounder's cell door. "That might be him now," said Ray. They looked under the crack of the door and saw four little tiny vole feet.

"Hornco, is that you?" The shadow disappeared and through a crack in the wall appeared Hornco. Flounder picked Hornco up and began to whisper in his ear. Hornco nodded, pointed, shook his head, and even gave a thumbs up. Flounder went back to the large main crack in the ceiling.

"I've communicated the secret plan to Hornco," said Flounder. "He didn't shrug?" asked Margarine.

"Of course not. ¿Entiendes el plan, verdad?" as he looked at Hornco.

"Si, perfectamente," said Hornco.

"What? Hornco talks?" Margarine yelled in excitement.

"Of course, he talks. Why would you think he doesn't talk?" asked Flounder.

"Well, every time I talk or ask him something he always shrugs," said Margarine.

"Did you ask him in Spanish? He doesn't speak English,"

"What? He's Spanish?" said Margarine in shock.

"Of course he is. You never noticed his little Cordoba hat?" said Flounder.

"Ella me habla todo el tiempo, pero nunca entiendo," said Hornco.

"What did he say?" asked Margarine.

"He said that you talk to him all the time, but he never understands you," said Flounder.

"Can we please keep this meeting on track?" asked Mrs. Warwick.

"You're right, Mrs. Warwick. Can we have a vote on Plan A, Plan B, or Plan Sea?" asked Ray. "All in favor plan A, whistle into your crack."

The only whistle he could hear was the wind blowing through the dungeon. "Plan B, all those in favor." A few whistles could be heard.

"Plan Sea?" Everyone started to whistle. "The seas have it. By the next full moon, we'll initiate Operation L.E.A.F. with Plan Sea. We're going to be free everyone. Freedom," yelled Ray.

Chapter Sixteen

STATUS UPDATE

⌘

" It was so wonderful being outside yesterday. I was able to get all of the professor's journals. Even the one labelled bear sightings," said Mrs. Warwick.

"That's great," said Ray.

"What does it say?" asked Flounder. Mrs. Warwick opened the journal which only contained one page. "It just says, try not to sight bears," she said.

"That's great advice," said Flounder.

"Did I say it was so nice being outside the city walls last night? On the way back to the dungeon, I even stopped and snacked on some blueberries."

"Where did you get them?" asked Ray.

"Straight from the bush. Even my pet cat was still alive. He was so excited to see me."

"He didn't starve?" asked Flounder.

"No, he must have found some voles running around the house that kept him fed. He looked great," said Mrs. Warwick.

"I'm so very excited about tonight. I can't wait for freedom again."

"Neither can I. Has anyone heard from Captain Limb? Did he send the jay last night to Chef Will and First Lieutenant?" asked Ray.

"Let me check," said Flounder as he went over to Captain Limb's crack. "Captain Limb, did you send that jay last night to Chef Will and First Lieutenant about the butter?" he whispered.

"Yes," replied Captain Limb.

"Captain Limb sent it, Ray. This whole plan is really coming together," said Flounder.

"It certainly is," Ray said while rubbing his feet. "And these feet are pretty excited to get those tappers back," he smiled.

Down by the buttery, a fresh batch of salted butter was being churned by Chef Will and First Lieutenant.

"What did the jay say?" asked Chef Will.

"It was from Captain Limb. He said Operation L.E.A.F is happening tonight. According to the jay, they need enough butter to grease up forty plus prisoners," said First Lieutenant. "Forty plus? Do you know how much butter that is?" yelled Chef Will.

"It's a lot. I'd say near two thousand sticks?"

"How many sticks do we have in inventory?" asked Chef Will.

"Last time I checked we had about twelve hundred and six. "

"We're going to need extra help if we're going to stick eight hundred sticks by tonight. Go get Kent. We're going to need his slappy hands."

"What about our food situation? How did Hu and Ape fare last night on the food run to the Butcher Shop?" asked Ray.

Flounder went over to Ape's crack and whispered, "Did you get the food delivered last night?" asked Flounder.

"He kissed me," said Ape.

"What?" asked Flounder.

"He kissed me. Hu kissed me," said Ape.

"What?" said Flounder.

"Hu kissed me. We were loading up a few hundred pounds of peacock steaks into a wheelbarrow. I was getting all sweaty and I told him I was going to take off my schmock. The moonlight must have hit my face just right because the next thing I know we were kissing over peacock rump roasts," said Ape.

"Wow. That's great, I guess. Did you and Hu get a chance to load up The Queen Mary, the Cog with any meat?" asked Flounder.

"We sure did. Well, I mean, we kissed more while doing it. But we managed to make several runs back and forth. Pretty much cleaned out the butcher shop. We got peacock ankles, roasts, steaks, cheeks, and legs. "

"Any thighs?" asked Flounder.

"Nope. Thighs are disgusting. We also managed to get four hundred bluegills and three hundred blue fin tuna. All on ice. Loaded and stored on The Queen Mary, the Cog," said Ape.

"Thanks Ape. Let Hu know you both did a great job," said Ray

"Oh, I will. We're probably going to go back to kissing some more," said Ape.

"Great. Enjoy. See you tonight for the big escape," said Flounder.

"Jay, jay," said the blue jay as it landed in Ray, Flounder, and Mrs. Warwick's cell.

"Looks like we have a new jay," said Mrs. Warwick.

"Who's it for?" asked Flounder. Mrs. Warwick grabbed the blue jays' leg and tore off the message.

"It's for Ray. It's from his cousin, Toss. "

"Go ahead and read it," said Ray.

"Ok. Dear Ray. This is your cousin, Toss. I received your jay and am excited to have you escape. I have a nice castle style home I took from a non-believer. Everyone is welcome to stay. I can't wait for you to meet Boob," said Mrs. Warwick.

"Boob?" asked Flounder.

"That's what it says. I can't wait for you to meet Boob."

"Boob?" Ray thought for a second. "Did he say anything else?" asked Ray.

"Nope. It just says I can't wait for you to meet Boob," said Mrs. Warwick.

"He didn't leave directions on how to get to his castle style home?" asked Flounder.

"Nope. The last thing he says is that he can't wait for you to meet Boob," said Mrs. Warwick.

"Well. I'm sure it can't be hard to find. How many castle style homes can there be?" asked Ray.

"A couple hundred?" Flounder guessed.

"A couple hundred? No, there can't be. Either way. Once we arrive at Snurburrie, it won't matter. We'll be free and I'll be paradiddling down main street in my tappers," said Ray.

Just as Ray started to practice his paradiddle, Hornco appeared under the door clearly sweaty and distraught. Flounder ran over to him and began to have a discussion in Spanish.

"I hope everything is okay," said Ray to Mrs. Warwick. "I'm sure it's fine. I've never met a Spaniard that wasn't organized," said Mrs. Warwick.

"Have you ever met any Spaniards?" asked Ray.

"No, like I said, I've never met a Spaniard that wasn't organized or disorganized," said Mrs. Warwick.

"So, you haven't met any Spaniards?"

"Right," said Mrs. Warwick.

Flounder whispered something in to Hornco's ear and Hornco left through the crack in the wall.

"Everything alright?" asked Ray.

"Well. We could have a slight problem. Last night, Hornco did an amazing job of getting most of his tasks done. He hid the coffee that the guards usually drink to keep them awake. He replaced all the guard's napping cots with super comfortable pillows. He instructed the castle minstrels to play something called smooth jazz, whatever that is. We're hoping that the guards will be so tired they'll fall asleep and not notice us leaving. For those guards that stayed awake, Hornco was able to loosen all the screws and bolts in every door in the castle. We're hoping that the loose bolts and screws will cause the guards to become confused and obsessed with getting them fixed. That should divert their attention long enough for us to escape," said Flounder.

"This sounds like a great plan. Thank goodness you speak Spanish and Hornco is around to help," said Ray.

"Well, it certainly is a great plan. I'll agree. There is one issue," said Flounder.

"What? What's the issue?" asked Ray.

"Well, Hornco was able to loosen all the bolts and screws in every door except The Queen Mary's bedroom. After loosening nearly six hundred bolts and screws, he simply ran out of steam and didn't have the energy to loosen her door," said Flounder.

"Hornco did a great job. Surely one door can't hurt. Plus, The Queen Mary will be sleeping. What could possibly keep her up at night?" said Ray.

****

"It's good to be Queen," said The Queen Mary while sitting in her tub full of hot water. "Margarine. More hot water. Post Haste," she yelled. Margarine ran down the hall to get a large kettle of hot water boiling over the small fireplace in the castle wall. "You realize, Margarine, it's only two hundred and ninety-two more days until my birthday? That day is such a wonderful day, don't you think?" asked The Queen Mary.

"It surely is. I wish my birthday was on your birthday," said Margarine.

"I'm sure everyone wishes they had the same birthday as me," said The Queen Mary. "Margarine. That gives me a great idea. Doesn't really surprise me, considering I'm practically divine," said The Queen Mary as she stood up and stepped out of the tub. "What if everyone in the city of Blueburrie had the same birthday as me? Wouldn't that be wonderful? What a lovely surprise everyone would have if I changed everyone's birthday to MY birthday, February 30th. Yes, this is such a wonderful idea. Margarine, tonight will be the night I announce my birthday switching plans. I'll start with the prisoners and tell the rest of my friends in Blueburrie tomorrow. I'm so excited. I'm not even going to be able to sleep tonight. The stroke of midnight. Yes. I will surprise all the prisoners at the stroke of midnight with their new birthdays," said The Queen Mary.

Margarine gulped.

Chapter Seventeen

THE STROKE OF MIDNIGHT

❧

"It's 11:30 wiggle the handle," said Ray. Flounder went over the cell door and grabbed the handle.

"Cross your eyes for luck," said Flounder. He grabbed the handle and began to wiggle. "It's still locked," said Flounder.

"Try clockwise," said Ray. Flounder turned the handle clockwise and the cell door opened.

"He did it. Hornco was able to unlock all the cell doors," cheered Flounder.

"Shhh. Be quiet," said Ray. Flounder quietly opened the cell door and saw several other cell doors open.

"Where are the guards?" asked Ray.

"The pillows must have worked. Look. There's a guard sleeping now," Ray pointed at a nearby guard fast asleep in his cot. "Let Operation L.E.A.F. begin."

****

First Lieutenant, Chef Will, and Kent loaded the last stick of butter into the massive four wheeled wheelbarrow.

"That's two thousand and two sticks. Hopefully this will be enough," said Kent.

"This isn't going to be easy. This wheelbarrow is heavy," said Chef Will.

"We have to try. They are depending on us to deliver this butter before the stroke of midnight," said First Lieutenant.

"Good thing the castle is downhill from us. Now, once we get this baby full of butter movin' there's going to be no stopping her," said Chef Will.

"Ready? Push," yelled First Lieutenant. The huge wheelbarrow began to creak and snap. It moved forward and started rolling faster and faster downhill.

"We're going to lose control," yelled First Lieutenant.

"Don't let go," Chef Will screamed, while holding on for dear life. Both men, each holding a handle of the wheelbarrow were now being dragged down Fourth Avenue towards the castle.

"Hang tight. We're almost there," cried First Lieutenant.

"I knew I should have greased my knees," said Chef Will while being dragged down the street.

"My slacks are getting full of peacock shit," screamed First Lieutenant.

Kent, knowing that he could easily outrun them, ran ahead and arrived at the Castle walls. I'm going to need something to slow these guys down. They're out of control, he thought. Nearby was a flock of peacocks roosting in a blueberry bush. Perfect, he thought. He grabbed several sleeping peacocks and lined them up on Fourth Avenue. "This should slow them down," he said to himself. Kent stepped aside and watched as the wheelbarrow full of two thousand and two sticks of butter came crashing down the hill towards the lined-up peacocks.

"Help us," screamed Chef Will as the wheelbarrow hit the first, second, third, fourth, fifth, and sixth peacock. Slowing with each peacock, the wheelbarrow finally came to rest by the thirty-second bird.

"You saved us," said First Lieutenant.

"You're right. Now it's time to save them," pointing at the dungeon walls.

"Let's get this butter moving," said First Lieutenant.

Running down the halls as quietly as they could, Pom, Gil, and Margarine ran towards the door labelled back.

"Good luck finding those tappers. I'll meet you at The Queen Mary, the Cog," said Margarine. She kissed Pom and Gil on the ear for luck and closed the door behind them.

"Hornco, you must get back to Ray and the other prisoners. You have to warn them about The Queen Mary's plans to change their birthdays. She's going to announce those plans tonight at the stroke of midnight. If she spots them sneaking out the window, the whole plan will be ruined," Margarine said. Hornco simply shrugged.

"This is important Hornco. You need to tell Ray," she said. Hornco began to run up the long hallway.

****

"¿Ella no entiende que soy español? No puedo entenderla," Hornco said to himself and ran up the long hallway to the dungeon.

"I need everyone to be quiet" Ray said by now everyone has gathered in Cell 9 which was the closest cell to ground level.

"When we get the butter, we'll start to grease up the bars of this window," said Flounder.

"Grease up the bars? I thought you said we're supposed to grease up each other?" said Captain Limb.

"I sent a jay yesterday that we needed enough butter to grease up about forty plus prisoners," said Captain Limb.

"What?" said Ray.

"Forty plus prisoners? That's too much butter. We're going to have an over-abundance of butter," Flounder said. Just as Flounder began to become frustrated a stick of butter flew through the cell window and landed on the floor beside him.

"There's the butter now," said Captain Limb. Ray and Flounder looked out the window to find Chef Will, First Lieutenant, and Kent throwing sticks of butter at the window as fast as they could.

"Look Ray. Their accuracy is terrible. They keep hitting the side of the wall. There's got to be eight hundred sticks around the outside of the window," said Flounder.

"Our accuracy. It's terrible," yelled First Lieutenant.

"Keep throwing. We only need one more stick," said Ray as he unwrapped the first stick of butter and began to grease up the bars on the window.

The sound of sticks of butter continued to slap against the side of the dungeon wall. "We only need one more stick," said Ray.

"What time is it? Are the guards still asleep?" asked Flounder.

"It's 11:55. No signs of any guards," said Dr Dunston who was keeping a watchful eye out.

"Ray. If we don't make it out of here alive, I want you to know you are my favorite prisoner to be with," said Flounder. "Every day I wake up, I get super excited about what adventures await us. It's been that way for years. I couldn't think of a better person to walk upright on this horizonal flat earth than you. You're my friend," Flounder said starting to tear up.

"Friend? But The Queen Mary, she doesn't allow it," said Ray. "I don't give a damn about her. We are friends," said Flounder.

"We are friends. Best Friends," said Ray as a stick of butter came flying through the cell window. Both looked at that golden stick of butter and said, "Friend, get that window greased. We're getting out of here."

Ray and Flounder stood on each side of the cell window with a line of prisoners between them.

"Next," Ray whispered and pushed the deckhand through the window.

"Me Free," he yelled as he squeezed through and fell several feet to the ground now covered in sticks of butter.

"Be careful. It's slippery," said First Lieutenant. One by one Ray and Flounder helped the prisoners through the cell window.

"Ape, It's your turn. Squeeze through," said Ray. Ape squeezed through the window and fell to the ground.

"Hu come kiss me. My lips are greased with butter," she said yelling to the cell window.

"Hu, you're next. See you on The Queen Mary, the Cog," Ray said.

"See you there," said Hu as he squeezed through the window and fell into Ape's arms. The two kissed and began to run down Fourth Avenue.

"Captain Limb, you're next," said Flounder.

"I didn't grease myself up," said Captain Limb.

"You don't need any grease. We greased up the bars on the window," said Ray.

"You think that will work?" asked Captain Limb.

"It's worked for the forty plus prisoners who just went before you," said Flounder.

"Ok, I'll try," said Captain Limb. "I need more grease," he yelled as he tried to squeeze through the bars.

"Quit spreading your arms," yelled Ray.

"Oh," said Captain Limb as he put his arms to his side. Captain Limb slid right through the cell window and fell to the ground where he was greeted by First Lieutenant and Chef Will. "It sure is nice to see you guys again," he said.

"Now, let's get to the ship and prepare for departure," said First Lieutenant.

"That's it. Just you and I," said Flounder.

"Best Friends. We really did it. We're really going to get the hell out of this town. I can't wait for all the new adventures we are going to experience once we get to Snurburrie," said Ray.

"I can't wait either. I can't believe how well this plan really worked. What time is it?" asked Flounder.

"Almost the stroke of midnight," said Ray.

"Well, after you, I insist," said Flounder. Ray stood up and pushed his arms through the cell window.

"See you on the other side of this cell window," said Ray.

"You bet," said Flounder. Ray fell to the ground and turned back towards the window.

"Your turn, Flounder."

The door to the dungeon sprang open and there standing was The Queen Mary in all her glory. "Announcing me," she yelled.

"The Queen Mary. Wake up prisoners. I have great news. I have decided that my birthday is the most important day of the year. And to honor that day, I'm changing all of your. . ." she stopped mid-sentence once she realized all the prisoners cell doors were open and the prisoners were nowhere to be seen. "Guards. Guards," she yelled. A few of the prison guards, who were sleeping quietly on their cots, sprang to action. "Guards. The prisoners. They have escaped. Sound the alarms. Run around frantically. Get me my prisoners back," she screamed. A guard ran to cell 9 and noticed Flounder now halfway out the window. He jumped towards Flounder and at the last minute was able to grab his foot.

"My fat foot," yelled Flounder. "Ray, he's got my fat foot."

"What?" yelled Ray.

"The guard, he's got me. He's pulling me in."

"What? This can't be possible. Flounder, wiggle free," said Ray.

"I can't. I can't. He's got both of my fat feet now," yelled Flounder.

"Flounder, no. Wiggle," Ray screamed.

Ray started to try and climb the dungeon wall back to the cell window. Unfortunately, the sticks of butter around the window made it nearly impossible to try and climb back up.

"Ray, he's pulling me in. I can't get free. I can't wiggle," Flounder yelled.

"Ray, I'm not going to make it. Go on without me. Go on to Snurburrie," said Flounder.

"I can't. I won't," said Ray.

"You must. You make people happy. So happy with your tapping. Ouch that's my thigh. He's squeezing my thigh. Really hard," screamed Flounder.

"I won't leave you. I can't leave. You're my best friend," screamed Ray. Suddenly Flounder was pulled in through the window and disappeared.

"Friend?" asked The Queen Mary suddenly appearing at the window. "I'm afraid you won't be seeing your friend ever again. Guards, chase them. Chase those simpleton prisoners. Get them," she screamed.

Chapter Eighteen

THE CHASE?

❧

"Your lips are so greasy," said Hu as he gave Ape another kiss. "Don't just sit there under that blueberry bush kissing," Ray screamed as he ran past them. "The guards. The guards are chasing us and they caught Flounder," said Ray. "We have to get The Queen Mary, the Cog. Regroup. Regroup," he cried. Ray now running as fast as his feet could carry him down Fourth Avenue towards the harbor. "I should have let Flounder go first. My feet are not as big and disgusting as his. He should have gone first. My best friend. He's gone. I can't believe it," Ray said to himself with tears in his eyes. "I know he would want me to go on but I just don't know if I can." He started to slow his running until he came to a full stop and looked around. "What do I do now? If I stay, I'm certain to die. The Queen Mary has said over and over that if we ever make any friends on our own, she'll execute us. She now knows about Flounder and I being best friends. She'll execute us for sure. I just don't know."

"Better hurry up. Those guards are coming," said Pom and Gil as they ran past Ray.

"Pom. Gil. Did you find my tappers?" asked Ray.

"Follow us to find out," they yelled, getting even closer to The Queen Mary, The Cog.

"Toss the lines and rachet the straps. Heave ho, boys. Twist and Tie those lines. Down with the buckets and let's get the hell out of here," yelled First Lieutenant.

"Hold that cog," yelled Pom as he, Gil, and Ray came running down that dock.

"Wait for us," screamed Ray. The Queen Mary, the Cog now slowly crawling back away from the dock.

"Jump for it," screamed a deckhand.

"Jump," Pom and Gil both jumped aboard.

"Jump, Ray. Jump!"

Ray looked around. "My best friend would want me to jump," he said out loud.

"Your best friend is me and you're going to stay right where you are," said The Queen Mary, seeming to appear from the shadows of the marina, surrounded by her guards. "Flounder is gone. You'll never see him again," said The Queen Mary with a smirk on her face.

"He's gone?" yelled Ray.

"He's in the deepest part of the dungeon, never to see the light of day," she said.

"Jump, Ray. Jump," screamed Mosh and Mrs. Warwick.

"Don't jump Ray. Your best friend doesn't want you to jump," said The Queen Mary.

"My best friend wants what's best for me," said Ray. "You're just a peabitch, with a peabrain. And you know what?" said Ray. "This peanis, wants to jump," screamed Ray as he jumped for The Queen Mary, the Cog barely grabbing on to the railing.

"That was a great line, Ray," said Mrs. Warwick, grabbing Ray's other hand and pulling him on board..

"I thought so. Now where's my tappers?" asked Ray.

"Turn that Cog around immediately," screamed The Queen Mary.

"Turn it around now," she yelled again.

Captain Limb, walked up from below deck. "What did I miss? I was sneaking in a quick nap," he asked.

"Oh, The Queen Mary is screaming at us to turn around." said First Lieutenant.

"She is. Well. Let's respond," he said. The captain approached the bow of the ship.

"Hey Mary. This is the captain, Limb. No," he said.

"Turn around immediately. Turn around at once or I renounce The Queen Mary, the Cog. If you do not obey, I will rename your ship. Your ship will no longer be named after me. Turn around or else," she yelled. Captain Limb took one look at the eastern horizon. "Boys. Raise the Sails. Toss the sculpture of the Queen on the bow in to the sea. The Cog is heading east. To Snurburrie!" The deckhands cheered and yelled.

"I really thought threatening would work," The Queen Mary said. She turned and headed for the castle, ashamed, and disappointed.

Chapter Nineteen

THE WORST CHAPTER

❧

"How are you doing champ?" asked Mrs. Warwick. "I can't believe he's not here. I can't believe Flounder isn't with us," said Ray.

"He's here. He's with us. His spirit is here," said Mrs. Warwick.

"I was reading through the Professor's journals and here's one labeled friends," Mrs. Warwick opened the journal and on the first page was a portrait card Floru had drawn of two small boys, and one of them pointing at the other boy's feet.

"Looks like two boys to me," said Ray.

"Those boys are you. You and Flounder. Professor Warwick always knew it. You two were best friends. Nothing but facts were ever written in his journals," said Mrs. Warwick.

"And Flounder knew. He knew all along. I could bring real joy to people's lives through the use of my feet," said Ray.

"That's the spirit," said Mrs. Warwick.

"Flounder's spirit," said Ray.

"Now let's find Pom and Gil. Get those tappers back where they belong," said Mrs. Warwick.

"Has anyone seen Pom and Gil?" asked Ray.

"Me thinks me saw them at the stern tossing old shoes off the back," said one of the deckhands.

"Old Shoes?" Ray gasped.

"Hurry. Mrs. Warwick. Come with me." The two ran to the back of the ship where Pom and Gil were casually laughing and giggling.

"Pom. Gil," said Ray, out of breath. "Where have you been? Did you guys manage to get my tappers?" asked Ray.

"Well. Problem is, we didn't," said Pom.

"What?" said Ray.

"We didn't. We were on our way to the community pond that night of the escape but noticed a bunch of uncut flowers along the way. We figured since we wouldn't be around for the next ball we should probably cut some for it," said Pom.

"Wait. So did you cut the flowers and then look for my tappers?" asked Ray. "No. After we got done cutting and organizing flowers, we spotted a wheelbarrow that needed greasing," said Pom.

"I told Pom that we should have grabbed some butter on our way out of the dungeon, but he didn't listen," said Gil.

"I know, I know. So, after looking at the wheelbarrow for a while, we decided to give up," said Pom.

"And then you went and looked for my tappers?" asked Ray.

"Nope, never did. That's when we saw you and started running towards the harbor," said Pom.

"Wait. So you don't have my tappers?" asked Ray.

"What tappers?" asked Gil.

"The tappers that are supposed to be on my feet," said Ray. "The tappers that make sweet tapping sounds when I paradiddle," said Ray. "I can't believe you didn't get them," Ray began to cry. "Mrs. Warwick. What am I going to do," said Ray.

"I don't know," said Mrs. Warwick.

Chapter Twenty

SNURBURRIE

❧━o━❧

"Morn ho. Eastward down. Ropes high," called out a deckhand.

"Good morning, First Lieutenant."

"Good morning deckhand," First Lieutenant said while sipping his morning tea. "How is The Cog this morn?" he asked.

"Cog is in top shape," said the deckhand. "Me love the new name. So much easier to say," said the deckhand.

"So much nicer to say too. The Cog." First Lieutenant smiled. "How many morns has it been?" asked First Lieutenant.

"It's our 30th morn at sea. Should be arriving at Snurburrie very soon. Me has me top deckhands on the lookout for land," said the deckhand.

"Very well. Let me know as soon as we arrive," said First Lieutenant.

At the stern of the ship sat Ray quietly picking dry peacock dung from beneath his toenails. "I wouldn't be doing this if I had my tappers," he said.

"How are you doing?" asked Hu and Ape coming up from the galley below.

"Chef Will made fresh blueberry waffles this morning, with peacock link sausages," said Ape.

"Very tasty," said Hu.

"Thanks guys. I'll probably go and eat something. I haven't eaten for a while. Just haven't felt like it," said Ray.

"You miss him don't you?" asked Ape.

"Flounder? I miss him every day. Every morning he would bring me my breakfast to my house. He never missed a single one. It was always fresh too. Never stale, never rotten. He was my best friend," said Ray.

"We know. Maybe try and eat something?" said Ape.

"Maybe," said Ray. Ray looked out at the side of the cog at the horizon. How was he going to live without Flounder? What was the point if Flounder wasn't by his side? Flounder and Ray had been together since they were very young. It wasn't going to be easy to start a new adventure without him.

"Ya hungry Ray?" asked Flounder standing behind him dripping wet.

"What?" asked Ray.

"I said, you hungry? You should always eat breakfast," said Flounder.

Ray turned and threw his hand up to block the sun. There stood Flounder dripping wet and holding a fresh stack of blueberry waffles, complete with peacock sausage. "Flounder. Is that you? What? Where? How?" screamed Ray as he stood up and hugged Flounder.

"Don't let go," said Flounder.

"Never," said Ray. "How did you? Wait. How did you manage? How did you get here?" asked Ray.

"I swam. What kind of Flounder doesn't swim?" he asked with a smile.

"You swam all this way? How did you escape?" he asked.

"Land ho. Off the port side bow stern," yelled a deckhand. "Morn the sails and cast the count jigs. Snurburrie ahead,"

"Snurburrie ahead?" both Ray and Flounder said in unison.

"It's here. We're free. I can't believe it. My best friend. Here with me," said Ray slapping Flounder on the back.

"I never gave up. Friendships sometimes can't be broken no matter what life throws at you. Every day I wanted to stop swimming, I just kept kicking. I think it was because of my oversized feet that kept moving at a great speed. Now. Finally. I'm back with my best friend in the whole flat earth. Looking up on a dream of new beginnings, adventure and more."

"Everyone to the front. Snurburrie ahead," Ray yelled.

"I have an announcement." The entire ship gathered at the front of the Cog as it got closer to the town of Snurburrie. "Flounder, my best friend is back. He survived the journey because of friendship. This made me realize we're all friends. Every person on this Cog is my friend. And we'll continue to be friends in our new city that offers new possibilities, new dreams, and more. Sixteen cheers for Snurburrie."

The crew of the Cog screamed cheers. Everyone gazed at the new city ahead. As the city came into view, it became apparent to each of them that opportunity was ahead.

"Look, Hu, there's a butcher shop ahead. It's for sale," said Ape while snuggling up next to him.

"Dad, you think they have a buttery in the town?" asked Margarine.

"I'm positive they do. I'm going to apply for a job, work my way up and name a butter after you someday," said Kent.

"Can Hornco come too?" she asked.

"Of course, he can. He's part of the family now," said Kent.

"Me Gusto!" said Hornco.

"What did he say?" asked Kent.

Margarine simply shrugged.

"They've got a master ballroom," said Mosh.

"That sign says Ball Manager Wanted," said Pom.

"Look. Wheelbarrow mechanic needed. See that sign," said Mosh.

"That's perfect," said Pom.

"You know, you will still need to apply for those jobs," said Gil.

"We know. But we've got the skills," said Mosh.

"I'm sure there's an opening for a city naysayer for you Gil," laughed Pom. Captain Limb stood at the bow of ship.

"Do you think they'll welcome us too? What will the Cog and its crew do next?" he asked.

"Look. There's a parking spot at the harbor. The slip says 'For Adventures Only.' I think that pretty much sums us up doesn't it?" asked First Lieutenant.

"It certainly does," said Captain Limb. "Deckhands. Head for spot 4, we'll be parking there" Captain Limb yelled out.

"I'm nervous," said Ray.

"Me too," said Flounder.

"I'm really nothing without my tappers. I want to bring so much joy to Snurburrie but without them, I fear, my tapping will come up short," said Ray.

"Everything will work out. We're together. That's all that matters. Everything happens for a reason, right?" said Flounder.

"You're right," said Ray. "Everything happens for a reason," he said. Just as the ship turned the corner to park in the slip a small store appeared up on the hill near the castle of Snurburrie. "Tappers We Are" the outside sign read. "Today Only. Buy one pair, get one pair free." Ray looked at Flounder and smiled.

"Tappers on me," he said.

"But I don't know how to wear shoes," said Flounder.

Ray looked at Flounder and said "Don't worry Friend. I can teach you."

www.ingramcontent.com/pod-product-compliance
Lightning Source LLC
Chambersburg PA
CBHW032014240626
47153CB00003B/1250